***The man she loved
might never love her, Claudia realized.***

For three long years she'd thought one day Joe
would look up from his desk and see her as he'd
never seen her before. Instead of being his right-
hand woman, she'd morph into someone sexy,
desirable.

He would suddenly realize he was in love with
her and beg her to marry him. She would tell him
she'd secretly loved him for years, and they would
live happily ever after.

That's the way it happened in fiction.

But this was real life.

And Joe Callaway was not about to fall in love
with her.

If it hadn't happened in three years, it wasn't
going to.

And if it hadn't happened the night of their office
Christmas party…when he'd…when they'd…it
was *never* going to happen.

Dear Reader,

Oh, baby! This June, Silhouette Romance has the perfect poolside reads for you, from babies to royalty, from sexy millionaires to rugged cowboys!

In Carol Grace's *Pregnant by the Boss!* (#1666), champagne and mistletoe lead to a night of passion between Claudia Madison and her handsome boss—but will it end in a lifetime of love? And don't miss the final installment in Marie Ferrarella's crossline miniseries, THE MOM SQUAD, with *Beauty and the Baby* (#1668), about widowed mother-to-be Lori O'Neill and the forbidden feelings she can't deny for her late husband's caring brother!

In Raye Morgan's *Betrothed to the Prince* (#1667), the second in the exciting CATCHING THE CROWN miniseries, a princess goes undercover when an abandoned baby is left in the care of a playboy prince. And some things are truly meant to be, as Carla Cassidy shows us in her incredibly tender SOULMATES series title, *A Gift from the Past* (#1669), about a couple given a surprising second chance at forever.

What happens when a rugged cowboy wins fifty million dollars? According to Debrah Morris, in *Tutoring Tucker* (#1670), he hires a sexy oil heiress to refine his rough-and-tumble ways, and they both get a lesson in love. Then two charity dating-game contestants get the shock of their lives when they discover *Oops…We're Married?* (#1671), by brand-new Silhouette Romance author Susan Lute.

See you next month for more fun-in-the-sun romances!

Happy reading!

Mary-Theresa Hussey

Mary-Theresa Hussey
Senior Editor

Please address questions and book requests to:
Silhouette Reader Service
U.S.: 3010 Walden Ave., P.O. Box 1325, Buffalo, NY 14269
Canadian: P.O. Box 609, Fort Erie, Ont. L2A 5X3

Pregnant by the Boss!

CAROL GRACE

SILHOUETTE *Romance*®

Published by Silhouette Books

America's Publisher of Contemporary Romance

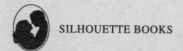 SILHOUETTE BOOKS

ISBN 0-373-19666-0

PREGNANT BY THE BOSS!

Copyright © 2003 by Carol Culver

Printed in U.S.A.

Books by Carol Grace

Silhouette Romance

Make Room for Nanny #690
A Taste of Heaven #751
Home Is Where the Heart Is #882
Mail-Order Male #955
The Lady Wore Spurs #1010
*Lonely Millionaire #1057
*Almost a Husband #1105
*Almost Married #1142
The Rancher and the Lost Bride #1153
†Granted: Big Sky Groom #1277
†Granted: Wild West Bride #1303
†Granted: A Family for Baby #1345
Married to the Sheik #1391
The Librarian's Secret Wish #1473
Fit for a Sheik #1500
Taming the Sheik #1554
A Princess in Waiting #1588
Falling for the Sheik #1607
Pregnant by the Boss! #1666

Silhouette Desire

Wife for a Night #1118
*The Heiress Inherits a
    Cowboy* #1145
Expecting... #1205
The Magnificent M.D. #1284

*Miramar Inn
†Best-Kept Wishes

CAROL GRACE

has always been interested in travel and living abroad.
She spent her junior year of college in France and toured
the world working on the hospital ship *HOPE*. She and
her husband spent the first year and a half of their marriage in Iran, where they both taught English. She has
studied Arabic and Persian languages. Then, with their
toddler daughter, they lived in Algeria for two years.

Carol says that writing is another way of making her life
exciting. Her office is her mountaintop home, which
overlooks the Pacific Ocean and which she shares with
her inventor husband, their daughter, who just graduated
from college, and their teenage son.

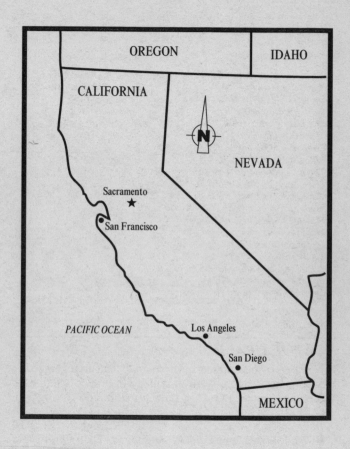

Chapter One

Joe Callaway was in a hurry. He brushed past the well-dressed men and women in the lobby of the high-rise building in San Francisco's financial district to be the first in the elevator. He punched the button for the twentieth floor and watched impatiently as the numbers flashed above the door. Three, four, five… It seemed like an eternity.

It was his first day back after what was supposed to have been a two-week business trip, which had turned into a much longer series of meetings, negotiations and public relations. He could just imagine the work piled up on his desk. Or the work that would have piled up on his desk if he hadn't had the world's most efficient, hardworking administrative assistant to handle it while he was gone.

The worrisome part was that he hadn't been able to contact Claudia from Costa Rica. Every time he had access to phone lines or the Internet, he got her voice mail. Every time he left a message, he didn't get a call back. Of course there was a time difference and problems with the overseas connection, still it was strange that he'd missed her every time. But she would have handled everything in his absence as well as anyone could have. After three years she knew his mind. Sometimes he found she could almost read his thoughts.

Now he was back and he was anxious to tell her what had happened. When she heard about the new project she'd be as excited as he was. They would work together on it as they had so often in the past, from early morning to long into the evening. The difference was that this project was extraspecial. Special to him, special to her.

He couldn't wait to tell her. He could imagine the expression on her face. Her brown eyes would widen in disbelief. Her mouth would curve into a smile. She'd pelt him with eager questions, how, when, where, how much. He smiled to himself as he rushed out of the elevator and into the offices of Callaway Coffee.

"Good morning, Mr. Callaway," said the receptionist as she swiveled around in her chair to face him. "Welcome back."

"Thank you, Janice," he said. "Would you send Claudia in to see me right away?"

He didn't wait for her answer. He wanted to get the papers out of his briefcase and onto the large work table before she came in. He was glad that he hadn't been able to speak to her before this. The surprise would be all the sweeter when he told her in person. When she was excited, her face would glow, her skin would turn the color of pink roses and be just as soft. Which reminded him of the Christmas party where she'd…where they'd… The smile on his face faded. That was something else he had to speak to her about. Just so there weren't any misunderstandings about that. Because he'd never do anything that would harm their wonderful working relationship.

It was now nine-fifteen and he was ready. Where was she? He wanted to see her now. He opened the door to the outer office. Two women from bookkeeping, Angela and Mary Lynn, were standing at the reception desk talking to Janice in hushed voices.

When they saw him, they jumped like scared rabbits and left immediately, their coffee cups forgotten on the receptionist's desk. Janice forced a brief smile, as if nothing was wrong. But it was. Claudia never kept him waiting. She was always there when he needed her.

"What happened?" he asked. "Where's Claudia?"

"I don't know," she said.

"What do you mean you don't know? Is she out sick? Is she late? Is she in the bathroom?"

"I, uh, I don't know. I haven't seen her."

"Haven't seen her? Well, if you haven't, who has?" he demanded.

She shrugged.

"Call her at home," he said.

"I tried. She's not there," Janice said.

"Not there?" he repeated. He had to bite his tongue to keep from asking once again where she was. He was beginning to sound like a parrot. But without her he was at a loss. Nothing would work. He couldn't function. He didn't know where to start. Didn't know where anything was.

"This is ridiculous," he said. "There's no reason to worry," he told himself, but he was worried. It wasn't like her to be late. Especially on his first day back. "I guess she's just late."

Janice didn't say anything. She blinked nervously.

"Isn't she?" he prompted.

"I think… Did you look on your desk? I think she left you a note."

A note? A note meant bad news. A feeling of apprehension tugged at the corners of his mind. He stared at Janice for a long moment then he turned on his heel and went back to his office. He hadn't seen anything on his desk except an avalanche of unopened mail and a stack of file folders, which, come to think of it, was pretty strange. He shuffled through the mess, knocking some things on the floor, tossing others to one side until he saw it. Under the papers he found a white, legal-size envelope with his name written on it in blue pen in her neat handwriting. He ripped it open, a feeling of foreboding in the pit of his stomach like a gathering storm.

Dear Joe,
I'm sorry I had to leave so suddenly while you were away, but something came up. I did give two weeks' notice, and I trained Lucy, the woman the agency sent over, so you should be fine. Best wishes with all the new projects and so forth.

Yours sincerely,
Claudia.

Joe stood absolutely still, gripping the paper between stiff fingers and staring in disbelief at the words in front of him. What had he ever done to her to make her treat him so cavalierly? As if they were boss and employee, nothing more. When all along he'd thought of them as a team. He was hurt, angry and stunned as he stood in his quiet office, the faint whir of the fax machine in the corner the only sound.

He wanted to yell, to shout, to pound his fists on the desk, to demand that she return, to ask her how she could do that to him after all they'd been through together, but he forced himself to be calm. He'd learned long ago, the hard way, to control his temper. This wasn't the worst thing that had ever happened to him. He'd faced catastrophes before. The year the coffee crop was wiped out in Venezuela, the day he was fired from his first job for insubordination. Of course there was always the corker, the time his parents dumped him on the steps of the military academy because they couldn't be bothered taking care of a boy they called a hell-raiser.

He'd gotten over those hurdles; he'd get through this one. First he had to find Claudia and persuade her to come back. Whatever she wanted, he'd give her—a raise, more vacation time, an assistant, whatever. Whatever had come up, he'd take care of it. He went straight to her office and opened the door. It was dark and silent. There was a faint hint of her floral scent in the air. But the only sign of life was the tall cactus plant he'd given her for Christmas on the windowsill with a red ribbon around the pot. If everything was chaos in his office, hers was the model of order and neatness. It looked as if no one had been in it for weeks. He felt hollow inside, as empty as her office was. He closed the door and went back to the reception desk.

This time he stopped to ask Janice a different question in his most level, calmest voice.

"Where's Lucy?"

"Lucy, the woman from the agency?" she asked.

"Yes, that Lucy. Where the hell is she?"

Janice's eyes widened. "She quit. She couldn't get used to the system."

"I see," he said, his jaw so tight he was afraid he wouldn't be able to open it wide again. "Could you call the agency and get a replacement for her, immediately?"

"Of course. Right away. I would have done it sooner, but I thought…" Her voice trailed off and he never knew what she thought.

He went back to his office where he sank into the chair behind his desk, leaned back and closed his eyes. Joe Callaway was not given to fantasy, but just for a moment he let himself think about Claudia and pretend she was still there.

The smell of coffee would be in the air, Callaway double French roast that she brewed first thing when she arrived in the morning. By now she'd be sitting across the room on the leather couch, her long legs crossed as she told him exactly what she thought about his latest idea, whether it was a new blend or a new store or a new marketing plan. She was the only one in the whole damn company he could trust to give him an honest opinion. A small smile crossed his lips as he thought of the many times she'd taken the opposite view. They would go back and forth, sometimes arguing nonstop, sometimes sharing a laugh. Then he thought about the Christmas party, and the smile on his face faded. This disappearing act couldn't have anything to do with…naaah.

He sat up straight, picked up her letter and read it again and again. Finally he folded it into the shape of a classic paper airplane and threw it across the room. It landed in the wastebasket. There, that felt better. If she didn't want to work for him, he'd get along without her. He got along before she came— when was that, about the time of the last earthquake?—and he'd do so again.

There was a knock on the door. He jumped up, his heart pounding. She was back. He sat down again, put his feet up on his desk and took out a cigar. He didn't want to look too concerned, like he was panicked she wouldn't come back when he knew she would. He didn't want her to think she was indispensable, because she wasn't. He didn't light the cigar, he just clenched it in his teeth.

"Come in."

It wasn't Claudia. It was Janice with a middle-aged woman in a business suit and sensible walking shoes. He put the cigar away and let his feet fall to the floor with a loud thud.

"This is Sarah McDuff," the receptionist said. "From the agency."

"Already? Thank you, Janice. Come on in, Ms. McDuff, and sit down. I have a feeling you're going to work out just fine," he said with a forced smile.

The problem was, no matter how good she was, there was no one to show her what to do. And Joe had no time to train her, even if he could. He had a meeting to go to so he left the woman alone in Claudia's office.

"I need to access the files on the Costa Rica project," he said, waving his hand at the computer on Claudia's desk. "Print out everything you can find." She nodded, took off her sweater and sat down at Claudia's desk.

He stood in the doorway for a moment, staring at the woman behind the desk who wasn't Claudia, trying to get used to the idea that she might not come back. But he couldn't. His whole world had been knocked over and tilted at a forty-five-degree angle. He was surprised to see the furniture standing upright, yet it was.

He knew he ought to give the poor woman more direction, but there was only one person who could tell her what to do and how to do it, and she'd disappeared. So they said. Maybe Janice hadn't really tried to find Claudia. Maybe Claudia had been hit by a bus and was lying unconscious in a hospital somewhere with amnesia. The thought made him feel sick.

He told Janice to cancel the meeting, and he spent the rest of the morning on the phone calling, learning that her phone number had been disconnected. Then he tried every police station, every hospital and even the morgue. He only looked up once when the woman, Sarah, came in to ask him what his password was so she could access his files. He had no idea. He must have known at one point, but that was the kind of thing that only Claudia knew. He told the temp to take the rest of the day off at full pay and to come back tomorrow.

Then he left the building and drove to the address on Claudia's personnel file. Funny he'd never known where she lived. He rang the bell at the Victorian duplex on Greenwich Street, and the landlady came to the door. She said Claudia had moved out two weeks ago.

"Forwarding address?" he said.

She shook her head. "Nice girl. Always paid her rent on time. She's not in trouble, is she?"

Joe shook his head.

"You her boyfriend?" she asked, giving him a long look.

"No, I'm not." He paused. "Does she have a boyfriend?" he asked, shocked at the idea. She'd never said anything about a boyfriend, but then he'd never asked.

"Pretty girl like that?" the landlady said. Then she pursed her lips. "I wouldn't know. I don't pry into my tenants' lives."

He nodded grimly and thanked her for her time.

He didn't know what to do or where to go next. There was so much to be done at the office, but he couldn't face it, not without Claudia. He left his car in front of her former house and walked slowly down the street to a coffee shop where the sign in the window said "We Serve Callaway Coffee" and ordered a double espresso. He sat outside at a table on the sidewalk, one hand wrapped around the cup, and stared off into space. Was it only a few hours ago he'd bounded into the office full of good news and plans for the future of the company? Now the future seemed dim and the new deal out of reach.

He told himself to get a grip. Nothing had happened. He was still in charge of a multimillion-dollar company. He had a great apartment overlooking the bay, a new car, a boat, a membership in the premier health club. He didn't need anybody. And yet…and yet…

He drained his cup, left some money on the table and left. He had to get back to the office for a meeting with the head of the hot new PR firm he'd hired. He'd called them while he was gone to find they were so much in demand and so busy they had to schedule the meeting with him and the art director for six o'clock this evening. Unless she, too, had disappeared. He'd better call and make sure they were still on. If they weren't, he'd go to his club and pick up a game of racket ball the way he usually did on Tuesdays. He could use a little strenuous exercise. He felt like a wire stretched taut under about two hundred pounds of pressure. A workout would help. Slamming a ball into a concrete wall would feel good. But the only way to get things back to normal was to find her.

Claudia Madison stood on the sidewalk looking up at the high-rise office building where she'd worked for the past three years. It was almost six-thirty and some of the windows on the twentieth floor were still lit, but that was probably because of the cleaning staff. Joe Callaway never worked late on Tuesday night, that was the night he went to his health club.

She'd been standing there for about a half hour, shivering in the brisk wind that blew scraps of paper around her ankles, watching, just in case. She didn't see him come out, she didn't see anybody she knew, thank heavens. Not even the woman she'd trained to take over her job. By now she'd probably settled in and was getting used to Joe's quirks. He would have been back from his trip for weeks now, and he'd probably forgotten about her except when he couldn't find something.

She sighed. If only she could forget about him as quickly. But that wasn't going to happen. Not for a while. Eventually it would. It would just take a little more strength of character than she had right now. Her teeth chattered. It was too cold to stand out there any longer. And too nerve-racking. She pulled up her collar, took a deep breath and marched into the building.

She should have come back weeks ago to get the one item she'd forgotten the day she'd cleaned out her desk. But at first she'd felt too awful, both physically and emotionally. Not going to work had left a huge hole in her life. Not seeing Joe every day had been painful. She'd avoided everything that brought back memories of the best job and the best boss she'd ever had. She even considered leaving it there and pretending he'd never given her a Christmas present. Then there would have been no such moment as this. After all, why did she want to have something around that Joe had given her that would remind her of him every time she looked at it? But now she was better. She'd made some important decisions. She'd taken control of her life. She could handle it. She'd have to handle it.

But when the elevator shot up to the twentieth floor and stopped abruptly, she started to shake with fear. The what-if questions crowded her mind. What if he was there? What if someone else was in her office? What if it was gone? What if it was dead? She pressed her hand against the wall and tried to catch her breath. She was about to turn around and go back down when the cleaning lady waved to her and opened the door for her.

Claudia murmured her thanks and tiptoed quietly toward her office. One glance at the door to Joe's office told her she'd made a big mistake. A slice of light was visible under his door. She heard voices. Joe's voice and a woman's voice. They were talking and laughing. She froze. What did she expect? That he'd taken a vow of celibacy after what had happened between them? Not Joe Callaway. He was obviously entertaining in his office now, the same office where he'd…where they'd…

She should have come back sooner or not at all. That was abundantly clear. She was too close now to turn back. It had taken all her courage to get here. With any luck she'd sneak into her office, grab it and be gone in two minutes. Then she would never return. Never see Joe again. Never hear his voice, never write another Dear Jane letter for him, never make dinner reservations for him and his date at trendy restaurants, never order flowers for his girl-friends, and never hear him flirting and laughing with other women behind closed doors. She would do it. She had to do it. She would do it now.

Her desk was bare and covered with a fine film of dust. It looked as if no one worked there. What had happened in four weeks? What had happened to Lucy? Claudia knew she shouldn't dawdle, but standing there allowed the memories to come flooding back. The time Joe had opened his first Callaway Coffee Bar, he'd burst into her office, lifted her off her feet and spun her around, his strong hands on her hips. It made her dizzy then, it made her dizzy now just to think about it.

Automatically, without thinking, she took a tissue from her purse and swiped at the dust on her computer screen. The motes filled the air. She sneezed. Loudly. She pressed her hand against her mouth to stifle any further sound.

There were footsteps in the hall. She dropped to her knees and hid behind the desk. The door opened. The lights went on.

"Hello. Anybody here?" It was him. Her heart pounded so loudly she was afraid he'd hear it.

There was a long pause. She held her breath.

The lights went out. The door closed. She heaved a sigh of relief. Then she stood, went to the window and grabbed the cactus plant, the one he'd given her for Christmas. Contrary to popular opinion, cactus could not survive without any water at all, but would die if overwatered. That was why she couldn't leave it there. No one else would know how to take care of it. It had nothing to do with sentiment. She clutched the pot to her chest and slowly, softly, opened the door and peered out. Nothing. Nobody. She tiptoed across the floor. The light was still on in Joe's office, but there were no more voices, no more laughter.

She sprinted out of the door and into the hall. Miraculously the elevator arrived seconds after she'd summoned it. She was breathing hard, almost panting as she pushed the button to take her to the lobby. As the elevator doors slowly closed, her heart was hammering loudly in her chest.

Suddenly an arm thrust through the small opening, activating the sensors, and the doors opened wide. He walked in.

His mouth fell open in surprise. "You," he said in a choked voice. "What in the hell are you doing here?"

The doors closed and she was shut up inside with the one man she'd hoped never to see again. She swallowed hard, caught a whiff of leather and cigar smoke and black coffee and the essence of Joe Callaway, and her knees buckled. She wasn't ready for this. She wasn't ready to come face-to-face with Joe, who filled the elevator with his broad shoulders, his dynamic personality, his flashing eyes and his pent-up anger.

"I, uh, came to get my cactus. I was afraid some-one wouldn't water it or even worse, they'd over-water or…"

"You came to get your cactus," he repeated, glar-ing at her as the elevator took them down. "You came all the way up here to get your plant, and you walked right by my office without a word. You didn't have the courtesy to tell me in person why you left. No, you were more concerned about your plant…. I can't believe this."

"I'm sorry," she said. "I thought you were busy. I heard voices and I didn't want—"

"I *was* busy. I was in a meeting. But the meet-ing's over. Which you would have known if you'd just knocked on the door. But you didn't want to see me, did you? You were avoiding me." He braced one hand against the wall and let her have the full strength of his cold, blue gaze.

"No, of course not." Her voice shook just slightly. She knew he'd be mad. She knew he'd be upset. He'd told her more than once how essential she was to the company, but she knew he'd find out very quickly she wasn't indispensable. Nobody was. There were plenty of other administrative assistants who were smarter, faster and harder working. She thought Lucy was one of them. She'd interviewed many and chosen her.

The elevator came to a stop at the lobby. Thank God. She brushed by him as fast as she could, conscious of the warmth of his body and the fleeting touch of his cashmere blazer against her arm. She hurried out and headed for the revolving doors. She told herself not to stop, not to even hesitate. Just keep going and never look back. But he was right behind her. Before she reached the doors, he grabbed her by the arm.

"Where do you think you're going?" he demanded. "If you think you can walk out of here like that without an explanation, you're mistaken."

Still holding her arm in his viselike grip, he steered her toward the small restaurant in the lobby. The same restaurant where they'd had many an impromptu meeting over coffee and a Danish when they had to get out of the office and have a private talk. It was empty except for two men at the counter drinking coffee and watching the basketball game on the TV set behind the counter.

The waitress smiled at them. "Kind of late, aren't you? Haven't seen you two lately," she said. "I'm afraid I'm all out of Danish, but the soup today is beef barley."

Joe looked at his watch. "That sounds good,

Ginny. Bring us each some soup, a green salad and a rare steak.''

She was gone with their orders before Claudia could protest she wasn't hungry. Even if she was, she had no intention of having dinner with Joe.

"I can't stay for dinner," she said.

"Suit yourself. Maybe you don't have to eat, but I do. I've had nothing but three cups of coffee today and I'm wired. I'm also tense and irritable. Do you want to know why?''

She shook her head. She did not want to know why. She didn't want to know anything about him. She did admit he looked tense and irritable, his mouth turned down and his jawline taut. She felt a pang of sympathy for him and stifled a knee-jerk reaction to reach across the table and smooth the worry lines from his forehead. She knotted her hands in her lap.

She wanted to walk out of there right now, before the soup, before the salad and the steak, but she didn't. For one thing she was afraid he'd come after her. Joe Callaway had not become the founder and owner of a premier coffee company at age thirty-three by letting people get away from him without telling him what he wanted to know. That's what she was afraid of.

On the other hand, he'd never tortured anyone

that she knew of. No, his tactics were much more subtle, and she knew every one of them.

"All right," she said. "Tell me why you're tense and irritable. Would I be wrong if I said it has something to do with the coffee business?"

"Yes and no," he said as Ginny set a bowl of soup in front of each of them. Claudia had sworn she would not eat a bite. She would show him what she thought of his high-handed ordering of her dinner. But the soup, full of beef and vegetables and savory broth, reminded her that she had not eaten much that day either.

Neither of them spoke while they ate. When she'd finished, he glanced pointedly at her empty bowl, but he knew better than to remind her she'd said she wasn't staying for dinner.

"The reason I'm having what you might call a bad day, Claudia," he said, sounding somewhat calmer, "is that when I arrived at work today after an all-night flight from Costa Rica..."

"What? I thought you came back weeks ago." No wonder there were circles under his eyes. No wonder he was strung out. She smothered a pang of sympathy. He didn't need it. He didn't deserve it. Despite the lines and circles, he was still obscenely gorgeous with his coal-black hair that brushed the edge of his collar and his granite jaw lined with the faint shadow of a beard.

"I was supposed to, but that's another story. A story I thought I'd be telling you this morning when I got to work." He paused and stared at her for a long moment. She tried to look away but couldn't. It was those magnetic eyes that held her, stronger than any physical ties. Then his whole manner changed. Instead of shouting, instead of demanding, instead of glaring, he spoke in a low voice.

"I can't believe you would do that to me."

She blinked and crumpled her napkin in her fist. Tears sprang to her eyes. She felt as if he'd stuck a dagger through her heart. He could do it. He could make her feel guilty for something he'd done. But then, he didn't know what he'd done. And he wasn't going to find out.

"I left you a note," she said stiffly.

He pulled it out of his pocket and smoothed it out with his fingers. "Is this it?" he asked.

She nodded.

"'Something came up,'" he read. "'Best wishes,'" he continued. "That's what I get after three years of taking you into my confidence, of treating you like a friend instead of an employee, of giving you raises before you even asked?"

A friend? Yes, that was all she was to him. Even after that night after the Christmas party? Yes, he'd had too much champagne. So had she. That didn't excuse him from pretending it had never happened.

The next day she'd driven him to the airport to catch his plane for Costa Rica, and he'd never said a word. She was hurt then, but it wasn't until some time later that she made her decision to be gone by the time he returned.

"What about me?" she asked, leaning forward. She was suddenly indignant and determined not to let him make her feel guilty or bully her. "What did I get? Yes, you paid me well. Yes, you confided in me. But who fielded your calls from your irate girl-friends? Who made up excuses for you when you wanted to break a date? Who listened while you vented your frustrations?" Her voice rose, her pulse accelerated.

He stared at her, as if she was a dormant volcano that had suddenly come to life. "I thought you liked working for me," he said, his forehead creased in a puzzled frown.

"I did," she said, suddenly deflated. "But I can't do it anymore."

"Why not?"

"For personal reasons," she said. She steeled herself against his strong will. She made herself sit there and calmly continue to eat, as if the personal reasons had nothing to do with him. She knew he was watching her, evaluating her every move, but she went ahead and picked up her fork and speared a mouthful of lettuce laced with a creamy dressing.

If he thought he'd gotten the best of her, he was mistaken. She knew now she would never, ever tell him why she'd left. He could bribe her with food or money, he could torture her, but she'd go to her grave with her secret.

"What's that supposed to mean?" he asked.

"It means it's too personal to discuss with you." She pushed her salad plate aside. "Now, can I go?"

"Not until we've finished eating. You look like you could use some dinner. Have you lost weight? Are you sick? Is that why you left?"

"No, I'm not sick and I haven't lost weight. I'm just eating with you to be polite."

"Polite? *Now* you want to be polite? You think this letter is polite?"

"It was concise," she said. "I got you a replacement. What more did you want?"

"I wanted you," he said through stiff lips.

She felt the heat sting her cheeks. Of course he wanted her. Who else would do his dirty work, screen his calls from girlfriends left in the lurch, answer angry letters, scan his e-mail and anticipate his every wish?

"Your replacement left," he said.

That explained the dusty office. "I can't help that," she said. "But I'm sorry."

"No, you're not," he said. "If you were really sorry, you'd come back to work. Or do you have another job? That's it. Someone offered you more money.''

"No, I'm not working," she said. "Not right now."

"Then what in God's name are you going to do with yourself?"

"I don't know," she said. "I might try teaching."

"Teaching," he repeated, shaking his head. "I didn't even know you liked kids."

"Maybe it's time I found out," she muttered.

He frowned, but before he could reply, the steaks arrived, sizzling hot with mashed potatoes and peas on the side. Her mouth watered. All thoughts of getting up and marching out instantly vanished. She *had* lost weight. She hadn't felt much like eating. But now, for some reason, sitting across from the one man she'd dreaded seeing, her appetite had returned with a vengeance.

"I don't get it," he said, setting his fork down. "I thought you were happy here."

"I was, but I needed a change."

"Why didn't you say so?" he asked. "I can give you a change. I've got something in mind for you that you're going to love. Much more than being a teacher. As soon as we finish eating, we'll go back upstairs and I'll show you what I mean. You won't be able to turn it down, believe me." He picked up his knife and fork, stabbed a piece of steak and chewed vigorously.

Claudia did the same. She needed to think. She needed some protein to go straight to her brain. Why hadn't she prepared for this meeting? Because she thought it would never happen. Why hadn't she made up a really good career change to tell him? Like doctor, nurse, engineer…TV repairman, chauffeur… What would he be likely to believe? Her mind was blank.

What about the truth? No, that would never do. She knew exactly what he'd say. She knew he'd offer money and sympathy. He'd be solicitous. He'd be kind. He wouldn't mean to, but he'd make her feel like a charity case. Just what she didn't want. She'd sounded iffy when he'd asked what she planned to do, but she'd actually thought it out quite carefully. The money, the new career, the whole plan.

The only problem was convincing Joe to let her go. Now that he'd cornered her, he was sure he could persuade her to do whatever it was he had in mind. She'd need the strength of a tiger to fend him off. She'd seen him when he wanted something or somebody. He would let nothing stand in his way.

The only way was to tell him the truth. If she could stand to accept his sympathy and some amount of guilt money, it would solve everything.

He'd have to let her go then. He was a kind and generous man. If she knew him, he'd probably send her off with a big bonus and his best wishes and hopefully never bother her again. She knew him well enough to know he wanted no entanglements, no ties, no demands on his time or his energy that didn't have to do with Callaway Coffee. Hence the string of broken hearts he'd left among the female population of San Francisco society. It was worth a try.

She took a deep breath. "Joe," she said. "I have something to tell you."

Chapter Two

"I have something to tell you, too," Joe said.

"You go first." If she was really going to tell him, it would give her time to get up her nerve and formulate her sentences.

"You know your idea of funding efforts to make Blue Grotto coffee drought resistant? Well, they've done it. It paid off. This year's crop is going to be spectacular. And we have the exclusive."

"No. That's great news. I'm really happy to hear that, Joe."

"I thought you would be, since it was your brainchild. But that's just the beginning. Now we've got to sell it to our customers. That's where you come in."

"Me? I'm no salesperson."

"You said you wanted to do something different. You said you wanted to be a teacher. You can teach the salespeople how to sell the new, improved strain of Blue Grotto or handle the PR. You can do anything you want. Just come back. Be part of the team."

"No."

He didn't pause. He kept on as if he hadn't heard her. "It'll be like old times, you and me working together, you and me... What's wrong?"

Old times. She didn't want old times. She could no longer schedule dates for him or arrange weekends at posh resorts with the woman of the month. Not since the Christmas party. She wanted, *needed*...to get on with her life. Life without Joe Callaway. "It won't work. I'm not coming back, Joe."

"Now you're being difficult. It's not like you, Claudia."

"How do you know what's like me, Joe?"

He looked at her as if she'd lost her mind. But she hadn't. She'd found it, and for the first time in three years she was seeing things the way they really were. The man she was in love with would never love her. It had taken a cataclysmic event to bring her to her senses, but there she was, and there was no going back. For so long she'd thought one day he'd look up from his desk and see her as he'd never seen her before. Instead of being his right-hand woman and trusted confidante, she would morph into someone else, a sexy, desirable woman.

He would suddenly realize that he was in love with her, not just her mind, not just her organizational skills, but her body and soul, too. He'd beg her to marry him. He'd convince her that in time she'd learn to love him, too. That's when she'd tell him she'd been secretly in love with him for years. He would be stunned and deliriously happy. They'd float away on a sea of love and live happily ever after. That's the way it happened in fiction.

But this was real life. And Joe Callaway was not about to fall in love with her, not now, not ever. If he hadn't fallen in love with her in three years, it was not going to happen. If it hadn't happened the night of the Christmas party, it was never going to happen. That's what she'd finally gotten through her thick head. About time.

She had fallen in love with him so long ago she couldn't even say when it had happened. Was it the day he'd brought her yellow roses after they'd worked until midnight printing a report for the stockholders? Was it the night she washed the spot off his shirt so he could look presentable at the opera? Or the Saturday they shared take-out Chinese in his office? Or was it that fateful Christmas party?

The party in his office after the real party he seemed to have completely forgotten?

He narrowed his eyes and leaned across the table. ''How can you ask me how I know what you're like? We've been together for what is it, three years now? That's longer than I've ever spent with any woman. You're the only one I could put up with or who could put up with me, for that matter, for that long. Doesn't that mean anything to you? Are you really walking out on me for no other reason than you want to do something different?

''It must be something else,'' he said, observing her closely. ''It's me, isn't it?'' The look on his face made him seem vulnerable for the first time since she'd known him. He'd faced adversity before. She'd seen him bounce back in minutes from every kind of setback. But for once he looked unsure of himself. Her heart fluttered wildly. She steeled herself to hold strong. He was a grown man. He didn't need her sympathy. He could take care of himself.

''No,'' she said softly. ''It's me.''

''It doesn't matter if it's you or if it's me. If you really won't come back, if you're really determined to do something else, go somewhere else, spend your days teaching little brats to color in the lines and print their names on their papers, then all I can do is to beg you to come back long enough to help me find someone else and train her. Will you do that? Is that too much to ask after all we've been through together?''

She stared at him for a long moment, wavering back and forth. If that would do it, she wouldn't have to tell him the truth. If he'd really let her go at the end of a week or two. ''One week. But at the end of the week, I walk out. No questions asked. None answered.''

''A month,'' he said. ''It's not going to be easy to find the right person to take your place.''

''Two weeks,'' she said. Then she'd tell him. She certainly wasn't going to tell him until she was sure she wouldn't have to see him every day.

He reached across the table, grinned and shook her hand. ''It's a deal,'' he said. He kept her hand in his large, rough hand for a long moment, the hand that could pick coffee beans on a faraway plantation as well as sign huge deals. Even though her mind told her she'd lost the fight, for one brief moment she didn't care. Just having her hand in his made her feel so warm, so safe, so special so...cherished. The warmth of his touch made all her fears fade away. She gazed into his eyes and they sat there for eons while their coffee cooled in the cups in front of them.

''Now,'' he said at last, reaching for the check and breaking the mood. ''What were you going to tell me?''

"Nothing," she said, and pulled her hand from his.

Later, riding home in the taxi that he'd called for her and paid in advance, her cactus on the seat beside her, she looked out into the dark streets of San Francisco and had a sinking feeling that she'd made the second biggest mistake of her life.

Joe slept like a baby that night, for the first time since he'd left home so long ago, secure in the knowledge that Claudia was coming back. They'd agreed on two weeks, but if he knew her, and he thought he did, she was back to stay. Whatever was bothering her would be forgotten as soon as she got back in the swing of things. He couldn't believe she hadn't enjoyed working with him. Not that he was an egotist, but he thought he was a fair judge of people. He thought he knew her pretty well and he thought he knew what it would take to keep her there.

He would make some changes, though. He'd taken her for granted. For one thing, he would never go off on another business trip and leave her behind. That was when the trouble had started. He would take her with him. That's what he should have done this time. She would have loved seeing the coffee plantations, eating beans and rice with the workers, watching the volcanoes belch smoke against the blue sky, and swim in the azure sea.

He stood in the doorway of her office the next morning. The sun was shining through the windows backlighting her slender figure. Her cactus was back on the windowsill. She was standing at her file cabinet, her profile so familiar, he felt a hard knot in his chest slowly disappear. She was back, and by heaven she was going to stay back where she belonged.

From that angle and in her dark suit, she still looked thinner than he remembered. He would have to see to it she didn't skip lunches in order to stay in and work. He'd have to order in for her. Last night in the coffee shop he'd had the impression that she hadn't been eating regular meals. He would make sure she did from now on because he couldn't afford to have her get sick.

He cleared his throat. ''Hi,'' he said.

She turned to face him. Her face was pale but composed. She really was very lovely in a quiet, subdued way. However, there had been nothing subdued about her at the Christmas party. It had taken a few glasses of champagne for her to loosen up, but when she had... He really must clear the air about that night. Make sure there were no hard feelings or misunderstandings. He wondered again, did she have a boyfriend? With her looks? With her personality? Of course. She must have.

She dispensed with a greeting. No good morning. Not even a hi. She got right down to business. It surprised him and disappointed him a little. He remembered her sunny smiles, her enthusiasm, their small talk. What had happened while he was gone?

"I'm going through the files," she said, "looking at all the temporary employees we've ever had, thinking maybe one of them might…"

"Claudia."

She looked up and met his gaze. "Yes?"

"I brought you a cup of coffee." He set it on her desk.

"Thank you," she said, but she didn't pick it up.

"Can we talk?" he asked.

"I thought we were talking."

"About something else."

"Of course."

"Sit down," he said.

She sat in the chair behind her desk, waiting expectantly, her coffee ignored, shadows under her dark eyes.

He dragged a chair over to her desk. He straddled it and faced her head-on. He took a deep breath. This was going to be harder than he thought. "It's about the Christmas party."

Her face turned scarlet. Her lips parted but no

sound came out. He didn't know what to say. I'm sorry for what happened? He wasn't sorry. I hope you don't think…I hope you're not angry…I hope it won't change anything… Nothing seemed quite right. When these things happened with other women it was Claudia who made them right. It was Claudia who wrote the notes and sent the flowers and made the excuses. She knew better than anyone how much he'd avoided commitments. How fast he'd run when he sensed a woman was after him. How he'd shied away from the *M* word. Not that Claudia was after him. Just the opposite. She seemed cool and aloof. He just wanted to clear the air, the way he should have before he left on his trip. But he was hungover that morning when she drove him to the airport, and she was so subdued he assumed she was, too. But now was a good time, just in case…

"I'm afraid I had too much to drink that night," he said.

"So did I," she said. "Let's forget it ever happened."

He was relieved but slightly hurt. He couldn't forget it that easily. He still remembered the red dress she wore that clung to her curves, so different from the business suits he was used to seeing her in, the music, the champagne and the mistletoe. The smell of the fir tree and the smell of Claudia's perfume that filled his senses. But if that's the way she wanted it....

"Of course," he said. "If you're sure..."

"I'm very sure," she said. "It won't happen again."

"Not until next Christmas," he said lightly.

She pressed her lips together in a straight line.

"Just joking," he said. He'd hoped for a smile. Some sign that she took it as well as she appeared to. That what had happened between them wasn't going to spoil their working relationship, because no matter what she said, no matter how hard she tried and how many replacements she found, not one of them would be good enough. There was no one who could take her place. If she didn't know that now, she would soon. He was counting on many more years of their working together. He was counting on the fact that after two weeks she'd realize what he'd always known, that she was where she belonged right now. As soon as she came to that realization, everything would be back to normal.

"Meeting at ten in the conference room," he said. "I'd like you to get the numbers on last year's production in Latin America compared to our other suppliers in East Africa."

She stood up. "Okay, but I'm going to need some time to do the personnel stuff, track down people for you to interview."

"Oh, of course, sure, by all means," he said smoothly. Go along with it, don't let her guess he had no intention of having anyone work with him but her.

"What about a man? Would you consider a male admin?"

He frowned. "I guess so. Why, do you have someone special in mind?"

"No, I just wondered. You get along so well with women."

"As long as they don't try to pin me down," he said with a grin.

"Why is that, Joe?" she asked, folding her arms across her chest. "Why hasn't any woman pinned you down by now? The minute they seem interested in you, you run in the opposite direction. You've dumped every woman who ever wanted to get involved with you. Or rather I've dumped them for you. The letter, the flowers, the candy."

Yes, it was true. He had a commitment phobia. It didn't take a psychoanalyst to figure out why he had to be the one who left first. But that was another story. And one he intended to keep to himself.

"Isn't it obvious? I like my life the way it is. I like my freedom. You know that. I have enough responsibility running a company. I don't need any more. You know me."

She nodded slowly, but she didn't return his

smile. There was something wrong. There was a chill in the atmosphere. She disapproved of his attitude. If she had in the past, she'd never let on. Now it didn't seem as if she could keep her displeasure hidden.

"What do you want me to do? Get married?" He almost laughed at such a ridiculous idea. But she didn't think it was funny. He could tell by the way she looked at him. The cool gaze she leveled at him. There was something definitely different in their relationship. If it had nothing to do with what happened at the party, then what was it?

She didn't answer his question. The old Claudia would have come up with something, made some comment, said something to put him in his place. The new Claudia didn't seem to want to bother. She was way too serious, way too thin, way too pale. He didn't know what to do to break the ice. He finally mumbled something about seeing her at the meeting and left her office, left her standing there gazing off into space and left his question hanging there unanswered.

Claudia sat at the end of the conference table looking around at the faces she'd worked with for the past three years. Joe had announced her return, but he hadn't been quite as clear as she'd hoped about the temporary nature of her stay at the company. She almost interrupted to set the record straight, but why bother? She'd be gone in two weeks and he could do the explaining then.

He then moved on to discuss new products, talked about the new, improved Blue Grotto blend, and had marketing bring in samples for everyone to taste in small paper cups. The smell of the coffee made Claudia's stomach turn. She, who'd always started the day with a big cup of Callaway Coffee, had dumped the cup Joe had brought her this morning down the drain. This was worse. This was stronger and darker. She pushed her cup away from her, but the smell permeated the air. Her stomach revolted. Her head felt so light it was floating above her body. The room was spinning around. Joe's voice was droning on in the background. She swallowed hard. She had to get out of there before a disaster happened.

Without saying a word, she got up and almost ran from the room. Before she reached the door, she tripped on Joe's foot and almost fell. She was only vaguely aware of the shocked silence that settled over the room, the surprised looks as she rushed out, the gasps as she stumbled. She made it to the ladies' room just in time to upchuck her breakfast. She didn't dare go back to the meeting. Instead she went to her office and dutifully munched a saltine cracker from the brown bag she'd brought from home.

Slowly her stomach stopped rolling and settled down to almost normal.

She held her head in her hands and wished she'd never said she'd come back. This wasn't going to work. She knew it. She'd given in to him when she knew she shouldn't. She knew how persuasive he could be and she'd let herself be persuaded. Why? Because she wasn't really ready to say goodbye to him? Because she wasn't strong enough to break the ties of their long relationship? Whatever it was, she had to give him the two weeks he asked for. She'd promised and she wouldn't break that promise.

She knew he would come looking for her after the meeting. She knew he'd ask for an explanation. She had to have an answer by then. She grabbed her jacket and headed for the door. She told Janice she was going out for a breath of air. This time the elevator was full and not one of the occupants was Joe Callaway. She felt better already.

Joe stood at the window of his corner office, his hands stuffed in his pockets, and watched her cross the street twenty stories below. He'd ended the meeting, then gone to her office. She'd left. Damn it, there was something wrong. She was sick. That was why she'd left. Whatever she had, she obviously didn't want to burden him with it. But he had to know. He would find out what it was.

He went to her office. He leafed through her daily calendar of appointments. He saw a notation for an appointment with the name of a doctor, and he called the number. The receptionist told him all he needed to know in the first ten seconds. There was no need to pry into her records or ask the doctor any questions. All the evidence fell into place, and out came the only possible answer. He walked out of the office without seeing the puzzled looks of everyone he met in the hall or the reception area or in the elevator. His mind was spinning, wondering, speculating.

Like a robot he walked out onto the street and as if he was programmed, he headed for the small park wedged between two high-rise office buildings. That was where he knew she sometimes took a bag lunch. He found her sitting on a bench, her head tilted back to catch the rays of the pale winter sun. He sat down next to her.

She didn't say anything. She didn't acknowledge his presence, but he knew she knew he was there.

''Feeling better?'' he said after a long moment.

''Yes.''

''Is there something I should know about?'' he asked.

She shook her head.

''Sure?''

''Positive.''

"Nothing to do with me?"

"No."

"Then who does it have to do with?"

"Me."

"You're pregnant, aren't you?"

A tiny tear slid down her cheek.

"Damn it, Claudia. I'm the father aren't I?"

"Don't worry about it," she said, her voice suddenly calm as she looked at him.

"Don't worry about it," he said, shocked that she could even think such a thing. "I *am* worried about it. I'm going to be a father. I don't have the slightest idea how to be a father."

"You don't have to be," she said wearily. "Nobody's asking you to be a father. This is my baby."

"Your baby? No, it isn't. It's our baby."

She hiccuped loudly. "I didn't intend to tell you."

"What? Why not? You didn't think I could handle it?" he said.

"I know you don't want to be tied down. You've made that very clear. You don't want any obligations. Well, a baby is one great big obligation."

"I know that. But…"

"But what? Now that you know, what are you going to do about it?"

"I'm going to figure out how to be a father, because if this kid is anything like me, he's going to need one.''

''All right, fine. You can be a father, from time to time, on a weekend now and then. That ought to give you a taste of fatherhood. More than enough. That way you won't have to change your lifestyle. You can continue to date the flavor of the month and still be Mr. Man Around Town.''

''Is that what I was?'' Yes, he liked going out with friends, parties, wine tasting, art galleries. Yes, he liked having an attractive woman on his arm. But that was then, this was now. If he had to, he could make some adjustments because he was not going to be a part-time parent. He'd had one of those, two of them, actually, and he wouldn't subject his kid to that kind of atmosphere. He didn't wait for her answer.

''A taste of fatherhood is not enough,'' he said. ''I'm not going to be one of those dads I see with their kids on the weekends, trying to make up for not being there full-time by buying them fast food and expensive toys. That's no good, not for him, not for me.''

''Okay, you can be some part of his life. We'll work it out. But what if he is a she?'' she asked.

''She'd look like you,'' he said slowly, taking in Claudia's dark eyes, her soft mouth and her pale cheeks. A girl? What would he do with a girl? A sweet little girl with Claudia's quick mind and gentle manner. Who played with dolls and drew pictures and sat in his lap and gazed at him with solemn brown eyes when he read stories to her. What about when she grew up, wanted to wear makeup and go out with boys? The idea was disturbing and threw him into a spin. He understood boys, but how would he deal with a girl? Then he remembered what she'd said.

"*Some* part of his life or hers?" he said. "I'm going to be a big part. You don't get it do you? We're going to raise this kid together. We're going to get married."

He couldn't believe he'd said that. He hadn't intended to say anything of the sort. He hadn't planned to get married, ever. He hadn't intended to have kids. Not after the way he'd been raised. The words just burst out of his mouth before he could stop them. But suddenly it was the only solution that made any sense. His child, raised by a single mother and an absentee father? No way.

"That's not the answer, Joe," she said soberly. "It may sound like a good idea now, but once the baby comes and starts crying in the night and there are diapers to change and bottles to heat, you'd be sorry you ever thought of it. As you said, you're responsible for an entire company. That's enough."

"It was enough. Now everything's different. If you can adjust, so can I."

"Let me tell you a little story, Joe," Claudia said, sitting straight and tall on the bench. "Once upon a time there was a married couple who didn't get along very well. Initially they were madly in love, with all the heart palpitations, the excitement, the hearts and the flowers that go along with it, but after a few years of marriage, when reality set in, they realized they didn't have that much in common. She was bored, he poured himself into his business. They grew apart, but they didn't want to dissolve their marriage. They thought they'd give it a boost by having a baby. They thought a baby would bring them back together again. A baby would save their marriage."

"Did it?"

"Of course not. Any psychologist or any normal person with half a brain could have told them that. A baby puts a lot of stress on a marriage, even a good one, which theirs wasn't. But they wouldn't listen. They thought they had it all figured out."

"I suppose they got a divorce, is that what happened?"

"No, they stuck it out, for the sake of the child, at least that's what they always said when anyone asked. Until the child went to college, then they both breathed a sigh of relief, they'd raised her and now they could finally split up and go their own ways, which is what they did and should have done years ago. What a waste.''

''I see your point, Claudia, but these people are not us.''

''No, they're my parents.''

''So what are you saying? You wish you'd never been born?''

''Of course not. I'm saying getting married just because you're going to have a baby together won't work. No matter how good your intentions are. In the past you made it quite clear you had no interest in getting married, at all, to anyone. You don't love me and I don't love you.'' Claudia was proud of how easily the lie rolled off her tongue. She'd tell as many lies as she had to, to make Joe forget this idiotic idea. It would never work. He would never forget why he'd married her. In time he would resent her for robbing him of his freedom. How long would they stay together? Until the child went to college? And then what? She could see the future so clearly. Why couldn't he?

''At least my parents were in love at one time, or they thought they were. What have we got going for us, other than the fact that we're going to be parents?''

''What do we have going for us?'' he said. ''I'll tell you what. We like each other. We respect each other. We know each other. We're well acquainted with all our little faults and foibles. I know how obsessive you can be about details. You know how careless I can be, how I overlook the details and go for the big picture. That's why we're so good together.''

"That's not enough,'' she said sadly. If only it was. If only she didn't love him, faults, foibles and all. Then it might work. But living with him, sharing a baby and a life while loving him and not being loved in return? "No,'' she said. "I appreciate the offer, I know you mean well, and knowing you, I know how it goes against the grain, but the answer is no.''

"All right,'' he said. "We'll leave it at that for now.''

She shot a surprised glance at him. Joe Callaway giving up so easily? Impossible. He hadn't accepted defeat. Her turning him down had just made him more determined. That's how he always was. Determined to get his own way. When he wanted something, he never gave up. Well, this time he would have to give up. This time she could be as stubborn and determined as he was. Because she had too much to lose. Her independence, her self-esteem, control over her life, everything.

They walked slowly back to the office, each lost in their own thoughts. She believed...she hoped, that once the reality sank in, he would retract his offer. If he thought she would change her mind, he was dead wrong.

He paused on the pavement twenty stories beneath their office, faced her and ran one finger around the curve of her cheek. She felt her knees weaken. But not her resolve. Never.

"Are you sure you feel okay?" he asked.

Her temperature rose about ten degrees from just his touch. She didn't want to see the sweet and tender side of him. She wanted him to be grim and cranky and refuse to have anything to do with her or the baby. It would make things so much easier.

"I feel fine now," she said, proud of how calm she sounded. "I'm sorry I made a scene. I'll...I don't know what I'll say, how I'll explain what happened."

"I'll take care of it," he said.

She knew when he said he'd take care of something he would. He not only took care of explaining why she'd bolted from the meeting, he had lunch delivered to her office. A turkey sandwich with lettuce and tomato and a spinach salad with a vinaigrette dressing. By that time she was ravenous and ate every scrap.

At four o'clock he called her into his office. She took a yellow notepad with her and a briefcase full of papers for him to look over. By force of habit she took a seat on the couch, then she remembered the night of the Christmas party and the couch where they'd ended up after locking the door and leaving a trail of their clothes across the floor. Her face flamed remembering how wantonly she'd behaved. Now she was paying the price. So was he.

She stood and looked around the office. For a moment she felt like a caged animal. She was stuck, and she couldn't get out. Would she ever get over it? Could she ever forget?

"Sit down," Joe said.

She went back to the couch. "About the hiring of a new assistant," she said.

"I want to talk about something else."

She held her breath. Not the marriage idea. She couldn't discuss it twice in one day. She didn't have the strength.

"Do you have a doctor?" he said.

"Of course."

"Is he any good?"

"It's a she, and yes, she's very good. I have an appointment with her next week."

"I'll go with you. I have some questions."

"If you want to, you can write them down, I'll take them with me. Because I wouldn't know how to explain you."

"Explain me?" he said. "I'm the father. What more explanation does she need?" He studied her face. "Why? What did you tell her about me? I didn't exist? I wouldn't be interested?"

She shifted uncomfortably on the edge of the couch. "I told her you weren't involved."

"I wasn't involved because you hadn't told me."

"All right, all right. I hadn't told you. That was wrong. I should have. I thought you wouldn't care."

"You thought I wouldn't care that I was going to be a father? You don't know me very well, do you?"

She sighed. "I guess not." She'd certainly underestimated his interest in this baby. Maybe she had misjudged him. Maybe they could work something out. But it couldn't be marriage. Never, not, negative, nix.

"Go on, go home," he said, running one hand through his hair. "You're tired. I've kept you here too long."

"It's just...it's been a long day." How many more would there be like this? She didn't mind working, she didn't mind assembling fact sheets, crunching numbers, writing business plans, but discussing her future and the baby's future? That drained her of all the energy she could muster.

"I'm sorry," he said. He looked so contrite she couldn't help feeling sorry for him. He'd had a shock today and he'd responded very honorably by offering to marry her. When she'd said no, he'd shown restraint and a commendable interest in the baby. What more did she want from him? A small voice at the back of her mind whispered the answer. *Love.*

Forget that, she told herself. It's not going to happen.

"I'll be better tomorrow. Good night, Joe."

He got up and opened the door for her. "How are you getting home?"

"I'll catch the bus."

"No, you won't. I'll take you."

"It's four-thirty. You never leave that early."

"It's six-thirty in Costa Rica."

"You're the one who should be tired. Why don't you go home?" she asked.

"I'm going to my club and work out. Everything can wait until tomorrow. Meet me in the parking garage."

Chapter Three

The car was black, low to the ground, sleek and very small. The smell inside shouted out expensive new car. The music that came from the multiple speakers was soft and soothing.

"Watch your head," he said, holding the door for her as she entered the passenger side.

"Is this a new car?" she asked, ducking her head and sliding into the leather bucket seat.

"I ordered it months ago. I thought I told you. But I just took delivery a week ago. There's a huge waiting list." The pride and excitement in his voice was unmistakable.

"What was wrong with your old one?" she asked. As she recalled it wasn't very old and it was very expensive.

"Not fast enough," he said. "And the handling was a little rough. I've been wanting a car like this since I was a kid. The only reason I wanted to learn to read was to read car magazines, and I could recognize every car on the road almost before I could talk. If I wasn't in the coffee business, I'd design cars or sell them, at least."

She glanced at his profile. So there were still things she didn't know about Joe Callaway. Even after all they'd been through together.

"It's very nice," she said politely. "Very compact."

"Small is what you're trying to say," he said. "That's right. It comes from Italy and they only turn out a few hundred a year. It goes from zero to sixty in four seconds."

"That fast. Have you tried it?" she asked.

"No, but I'm going to test it on the weekend on a track in Monterey. Would you like to come along?"

"I don't think so. Going from zero to sixty I might throw up all over your nice leather."

"I mean to watch from the stands. Some of the wives do that."

"I'm not… No, thanks," she said, turning her head to look out the window. He wasn't going to start in on the marriage thing again, was he? "I'm going baby shopping this weekend."

"Already? What does he need, anyway?"

"Oh, things like a crib and a changing table, a chest of drawers, just the basics." She hadn't planned on baby shopping, but why not? It seemed like a good excuse for not watching Joe race around a track. Not that she needed one. He was her boss, and until the baby came, that was all he was. She owed him her time between nine and five and that was it. And after the baby was born…? Who knew? However determined he was to play the father role, she still thought he'd lose interest once he faced the reality of a newborn.

She leaned back in her seat and decided to enjoy the luxury of Joe's rare, Italian, compact sports car, with its two luxurious seats, as long as he didn't break the speed limit with her in it. He'd worked hard for the perks in his life; she knew that. If he wanted to share them with her, she'd try to appreciate them, too.

But that wasn't the only luxury he wanted to share with her.

"Shouldn't you be exercising?" he asked.

"I suppose so," she said. Right now exercising was the last thing on her mind. She wanted to sink into an easy chair and turn on some mindless TV program. All her energy had been drained out of her.

"I'm going to get you a membership in my health club. They've opened a ladies' section. You can swim, do yoga, have a personal trainer if you want. We can go together.''

''I'm only going to be around for two weeks,'' she reminded him.

''That doesn't mean you can't exercise after the two weeks are up. We'll ask your doctor what she thinks.''

Claudia closed her eyes. *We* can go together. *We'll* ask your doctor... Where would it all end? She felt herself sinking deeper and deeper into a hole until soon she wouldn't be able to get out. She'd be inexorably tied to Joe but not really. Not where it counted. He'd be a part of her life and yet he wouldn't. She'd be in some kind of terrible limbo. While he continued to date and make the social scene, he'd keep one hand in her life and her baby's. *Their* baby's.

She wondered how long it would last, this interest in her pregnancy and the baby. Until she started swelling up like a balloon? Until they started childbirth classes? Until he saw that the baby looked like a red wrinkled prune and screamed its head off from two to four every morning? Until it drooled all over his four-hundred-dollar suits?

She had her hand on the handle as soon as he pulled up in front of her friend Molly's duplex in Bernal Heights.

"Why did you move?" he asked before she could escape.

"To save money. I didn't know how long I'd be out of work so… Anyway, my friend Molly had a spare bedroom. I pay her a small amount every month and it works out fine."

Except that Molly talked a blue streak, gave advice a little too freely, had six cats and an omnipresent boyfriend. But that was none of Joe's business.

"Good night and thanks for the ride." She was on the sidewalk now.

He got out of the car. "Wait a minute. I don't have your phone number."

She wrote it on a piece of paper and handed it to him. Just when she thought she was finally rid of him, he walked her up to the door, his hand pressed lightly against the small of her back.

"Really, Joe, I'm fine," she said, the muscles tensing in her arm. "I think I can make it up to the door on my own." One more minute of his company, of his overly solicitous attitude and she might explode. If he kept this up, it was going to be a long nine months.

When she opened the door with her key, two of Molly's cats were waiting for her.

"Don't let them out," Molly shouted from the

living room. "Oh, I didn't know we had company," she said spotting Joe.

"We don't," Claudia said.

Joe didn't wait for the invitation that he was sure wasn't coming. He wanted to see how Claudia lived. He walked into the living room, held out his hand and introduced himself to Molly and a guy in jeans and a T-shirt who got up from the couch where he'd been drinking a beer.

Joe gave a quick cursory glance around the living room and took in the rumpled futon covered with cat fur, the fake leather recliner, the television with a sitcom on, a half-eaten pizza on the coffee table and the empty beer cans. There was nothing wrong with it, nothing at all. Plenty of single people lived like that with boyfriends and cats. But he couldn't picture a baby living there. Not his baby.

Actually he couldn't picture a baby living in his condo, either. In fact, children weren't allowed. If they got married...but Claudia didn't want to marry him. He wasn't sure why. He didn't really buy her argument about her parents and the right atmosphere to bring up a child. He was pretty sure a two-parent household was better than a single parent. He had to convince her of that. But how?

All he knew was that she looked so tired. He knew he should leave, but he wanted to smooth the frown from her forehead and brush away the dark smudges from under her eyes. He wanted to take her home with him to a clean, calm, empty condo, but she looked like her cactus, all prickly and stiff. He had the feeling he'd get stung by a thorn if he even reached in her direction. So he just said good-bye and told her to get some rest, which caused her to glare at him. He didn't know why. Was he being dictatorial? No, of course not. It must be her. It must be the hormones. And he left.

Joe went to the club and lost his game of racket ball, but he got some good exercise and some even better advice from his friend Andy.

"You're asking me how to get a woman to marry you? You, the man who has to fight off women?" Andy asked from the bench in the locker room. "Now you want to get married. I don't believe it. Who's the lucky woman?"

"You don't know her and she doesn't think she's lucky. She refuses to listen to reason."

"Reason? What does reason have to do with it? What did you say? How did you ask her?"

"I don't know. Something like, 'we're going to get married.'"

"No wonder. Women don't respond well to taking orders. They want to be coaxed, wooed, romanced. Candlelight dinners, music, presents. Hell, you know all this Joe. I can't believe I'm telling you this.''

Yes, he knew it all, but so did Claudia. She was the one who sent the presents. She'd be immune to the usual routine. She'd see right through it. ''This is different,'' he said. ''This is someone who wouldn't want... You think it will work on anybody?'' he asked.

''Anybody with XX chromosomes.''

Joe tossed a towel toward the bin and pulled his T-shirt over his head. ''So take her out, give her presents, that kind of thing?''

Andy nodded.

''It's worth a try.'' Anything was worth a try if it meant a chance to give his kid the home he'd never had and the kind of parents he'd needed. She thought he would be put off by a baby crying? She had no idea what he would put up with to give his kid the upbringing he'd never had.

He would start tomorrow. He'd sweep her off her feet. She wouldn't know what hit her. After all, she was a woman, wasn't she? With the usual needs and desires? He'd learned that much on their one night together. He wouldn't stop until she gave in. She might protest, she might resist, but in the end he'd win. He always did.

By the time he got home he'd decided not to wait until tomorrow. He had to get started. Time was of the essence. He had her number, and he would call her tonight.

"Did I wake you?" he asked.

"No."

"Did you eat dinner?"

"Yes, I ate dinner."

"It wasn't a pizza, was it?"

"No, it was seventeen grams of cod liver oil and a cup of raw broccoli. Are you satisfied? Are you going to check up on me every night?" she asked irritably.

"I'm actually calling about Saturday night," he said. "I know you're shopping, but I was wondering if you're free for dinner."

There was a long pause. "I thought you were going to Monterey."

"Not this weekend," he said. He could go to Monterey to test drive his car anytime. This was more important. "Well, are you?"

"No, I'm not," she said at last. "I'm baby-sitting for a friend."

"Oh." He had the distinct feeling she didn't want to go out with him and had made up an excuse. It didn't happen to him that often, and he wasn't sure how to proceed.

"What about Sunday night?"

"I'm busy."

"I guess I'll see you tomorrow then," he said.

"Goodbye."

So much for his new plan. He shouldn't have taken no for an answer. He should have kept her on the line, made small talk, found out if she would ever go out with him or if it was part of her new policy to avoid him outside of the office. Damn, this was not the way it was supposed to happen.

He looked through his small, personal black leather phone book and went through the names of various women he'd dated. No reason why he couldn't call one of them. They wouldn't be "baby-sitting" on a Saturday night or "busy" on Sunday. But he couldn't work up any enthusiasm for it. Couldn't even remember what they looked like. This was Claudia's fault. She'd made it impossible for him to resume his normal life. She wouldn't go out with him, but he couldn't go out with anyone else, either. Then he had an idea he didn't see how she could turn down.

He didn't put his idea in place until Friday. The week had been filled with meetings and a few interviews with candidates Claudia had lined up to fill her place, but he'd conveniently found something wrong with each of them. It wasn't hard—not enough experience, too young, too old, too brash, too timid. When what was really wrong with them was that they weren't Claudia, but he didn't say that. Each time he turned someone down, Claudia frowned, but she didn't give up. She just scheduled someone else.

Claudia kept looking at her watch on Friday afternoon. It had been the longest week of her life, working with Joe, watching him watch her, knowing he knew she was pregnant, knowing he wanted to marry her out of a sense of obligation. Knowing he'd do anything to get his way. She could hardly wait for the weekend so she could let down her guard and relax. At four-thirty, she decided to leave a note for him and sneak out early. Not that he cared if she didn't stay until five. He was always suggesting she take a long lunch hour or a nap after lunch in her office. He hadn't suggested another date. Hopefully he'd gotten the message. She would not be another one of the women in his life. To be courted and then dropped when he realized how she felt about him. She could conceal it at the office, but looking into his eyes across the candlelit table at an expensive and intimate restaurant? How about when he reached across the table and took her hand or ran his finger along the curve of her cheek? She wasn't made of stone. Whatever she did, she must never let him know how she felt about him. However many lies she told, it was worth it to escape his presence after work.

One week down. One more week to go. But how

could she leave before finding him a replacement? She didn't like the way he dismissed everyone she'd lined up for him. They were all qualified. She'd screened them first. But he'd found something wrong with them. If he thought he would keep her on while she kept trying to find someone and he kept nixing them, he was mistaken.

It was time to leave. She took her jacket and went to his office.

She knocked lightly on the door, then went in. He was leaning back in his swivel chair, his feet on his desk.

"Leaving?" he asked, noting the sweater over her shoulders.

"Yes, but Joe, next week, we have to find you a replacement. It's my last week. Remember?"

"Of course. We will find someone. Don't worry about it." He was too smooth. Too slick. He wasn't worried about it because he thought she'd stay. She wouldn't.

"Next Friday is my last day," she said.

"Uh-huh," he said. "Take it easy this weekend. If you can. Isn't baby-sitting kind of strenuous?"

"No, not really. These are good kids. I'll give them their supper and put them to bed. That's all."

After lying to Joe about her baby-sitting, she'd felt so guilty she'd volunteered to give her friends Al and Sharon a night off from their two children.

They were delighted and immediately made plans for a rare night out, so now her excuse was valid. She couldn't go out with Joe. She would never go out with him.

"I guess I don't know much about kids," he said.

"No, neither do I," she said.

"You must know something, if you're baby-sitting," he said. "I was wondering if I could come by and see how you do it."

"How I baby-sit?" she asked.

"Just see how it works. What the kids are like. How old are they?"

"Six months and four and a half years. There really won't be much to see."

"Would you mind?"

Yes, she'd mind. She wanted a Joe-Callaway-free weekend. Time to strengthen her resolve, so that when he asked to stay just one more week, and then one more after that, she could say no and mean it. Time to pull herself together. Time to regroup.

"I won't stay long," he said. His jacket hung over the back of his chair. His tie was loosened. His hair angled over his forehead. The sleeves of his shirt were rolled up to the elbows. He looked so guileless, so hopeful, so eager, so sincere, almost irresistible. But not quite. What if she had a little boy who looked just like him? Her knees got so weak at the thought she sat down in the chair opposite him instead of walking out as she'd planned. He smiled and her heart melted. How could she say no, when all he wanted was to observe her baby-sitting?

"All right," she said.

"You don't think they'll mind?" he asked.

"Al and Sharon? No, as long as you don't give the kids candy or play baseball in the living room."

"I'll just be an observer. You won't even know I'm there."

Claudia doubted that very much. She gave him the address, told him she'd be there at six-thirty and suggested he come sometime afterward. Maybe he'd arrive after the kids were in bed. He'd see there was nothing to see, nothing to observe. He'd be bored and he'd leave.

Claudia thought it was a good idea for her to see what taking care of a six-month-old baby was like. It wouldn't be that long before she had an infant of her own, and she knew about as much as Joe did about taking care of children, which was next to nothing.

When she arrived at the Tremaines' house in the marina, the parents were dressed and ready to go, but the kids were unhappy.

"You remember Claudia, don't you Kyle?" Sharon asked.

He shook his head and refused to even look at her.

"I'm really sorry he's so cranky," Sharon said with a nod at her son, who was tugging at the hem of her skirt and begging her not to go. "He might be getting a cold."

"He'll be fine as soon as you leave," Claudia said.

"I hope so. We'll have our cell phone, so if anything happens…"

"It won't. Come on, Kyle, let's play with your truck and your cars," Claudia said brightly.

He shook his head, put his thumb in his mouth and continued to pull at his mother's skirt.

"I left a bottle for Kristin in the fridge. In case she wakes up. But she probably won't. This is so sweet of you. Honestly, I don't know how we'll repay you," Sharon said.

"Don't even think about it. I've been meaning to do this for a long time. Just never got around to it." They didn't know she was pregnant. None of Claudia's friends did, not even her new roommate. It was too hard to explain how and who and what she was going to do about it. That time would come, but not yet.

"By the way," Claudia said. "A friend of mine might drop over. I hope that's okay."

"Male? A male friend?" Sharon asked, her eyes lighting up.

"Uh…yes."

"But that's wonderful. I only hope the kids will be asleep so you won't be disturbed."

"It doesn't matter. It's no one special." No one special. Just my boss. Just the father of my baby. Oh, Lord, if they only knew.

She waved goodbye from the window after getting the phone number of their pediatrician and more tears from little Kyle, who'd finally been pried away from his mother but who continued to cry long after they'd gone despite Claudia's efforts to distract him.

"How about some juice? Will you show me your room? Want to read a story?"

He shook his head violently to each question, then he ran down the hall yelling, "I want my mommy," which woke up his sister. Claudia sighed and went to pick up the baby. She went to the kitchen to put the bottle into the microwave oven. She had no idea that two crying children could make so much noise. Her head started aching. Just as she was wondering if the neighbors would call and complain, the phone rang.

Chapter Four

When she picked up the phone, the doorbell rang. Good heavens, how did anyone manage?

"Claudia, I forgot to tell you about the toilet," Sharon said. "It's been acting up. The plunger is in the closet in the hall."

"Don't worry, Sharon, I know how to handle it." As soon as she hung up she went to the door with the baby on her shoulder. When she got there she found Kyle had opened the door and Joe was standing there with a big box in his hands.

"Kyle," Claudia said. "You're not supposed to open the door to strangers."

"My mom lets me," he said defiantly.

"Hello, Joe."

Joe looked at Claudia, then at the crying baby and back at Kyle, who had finally stopped crying and was eyeing Joe and the box in his hands with interest.

"Looks like you could use a little help," Joe said.

"I have to get her bottle. If you could just do something with Kyle. Kyle, this is Joe."

She turned to go to the kitchen and left them. Yes, she could use a little help, though what Joe would do with the boy was questionable. Especially after Kyle had turned all her offers down.

The baby didn't want her bottle. Now what? She continued to cry piteously. Claudia felt helpless. She checked her diaper, patted her on the back, then carried her down the hall toward Kyle's room with its painted mural of dinosaurs and dragons on the wall.

There in the middle of the floor were Kyle on his knees and Joe with his long legs stretched out in front of him with at least thirty trucks and cars between them along with a plastic toy garage that had been in the box Joe brought. Now how did he know what to bring a five-year-old boy? Because he'd been one, of course.

Kyle was making roaring car noises as he pushed a truck up the ramp. He'd stopped crying and was engrossed in his toys. Hadn't she offered to play with him? What had Joe done that she hadn't? Why had Kyle taken an instant dislike to her? What if she had a son like that?

Joe looked up at her. "What's wrong with her?" he asked, meaning the crying baby. "It is a her, isn't it?"

"I don't know what's wrong. She wouldn't take her bottle, so I guess she isn't hungry."

"Let me try," Joe said reaching for the baby. Claudia hesitated only a moment before handing the baby and her bottle to Joe on the floor. He'd soon see that nothing worked.

"How do you do this?" Joe asked, holding the baby in his arms.

Kyle, looking proud of himself, showed him how to tilt the bottle, and Joe managed to get the nipple into the baby's mouth. She made loud sucking sounds as if she'd been starving.

Claudia stood in the middle of the room staring. Of course Joe would know how to play cars with a little boy. But how could a macho man who'd probably never even seen a baby before at close quarters succeed in getting her to take a bottle when she couldn't?

But Kyle wasn't happy with Joe's lack of attention. He started to whine. Claudia offered to play with him, but he shook his head and frowned at her.

"Okay," Joe said to him. "Move the trucks into the garage. We're going to race the cars."

Kyle did what he said, making zooming noises in the back of his throat.

Joe kept up a running dialogue with the boy while holding the baby. Claudia had never felt more surprised and more useless.

"Do you want to give her to me?" she asked at last.

Joe looked up. "I'm okay. Sit down, you can play with us."

Kyle snorted. "She's a girl," he said. "She doesn't know about cars."

Claudia shifted from one foot to the other. She couldn't refute that.

Tired of standing there, feeling unwanted and unnecessary, Claudia walked back to the baby's room and picked up a well-worn stuffed bunny from the baby's crib. She looked around the room at the shelves full of dolls and stuffed animals, at the pastel-colored pictures on the walls and the changing table and the mobile that hung over the crib. So much to buy. So much to do. How was she ever going to do it alone? Just thinking about it made her so tired. So terribly tired.

She sat down for a moment in the rocking chair in the corner, with the bunny in her lap, for a long moment. What made her think she could be a mother? She couldn't even do it for one night, let alone a lifetime. And after she'd criticized Joe for not knowing how to be a father. If she hadn't seen him in the middle of the floor playing with a five-year-old boy while holding a baby, she'd never have believed it. What did he have that she didn't?

Of course, as an only child, she'd never had a baby sister or brother around the house to practice on and she'd never baby-sat. But neither had Joe. She didn't know how long she sat there, daydreaming, worrying about being a full-time mother when she was having so much trouble taking care of two kids for one night.

When Joe appeared in the doorway, the baby still in his arms, she came out of her trance with a jolt. What was it about this big, broad-shouldered man in khakis and a sport shirt holding a tiny baby that made her heart throb? That filled her with a rising tide of longing and desire. Why, oh, why had she told him he could come there tonight? But what if she hadn't? How would she have managed?

"Sorry," she said, jumping guiltily out of the rocking chair. "I left you alone. Oh, she's asleep," she said lowering her voice to a whisper. "How did you do that?"

"I didn't do anything," he said. "I guess she just got tired. How do I know? What should I do, put her in her bed?"

"Yes." Claudia wanted to take her from his arms, to hold her, to smell that sweet baby smell and feel the softness of her skin, but she was afraid of waking her again, so she just watched helplessly while Joe put her in the crib. Then she laid a blanket over the sleeping baby and stood staring at her. There was a long silence while they stood there together.

Claudia couldn't help thinking that if she married Joe, it could be like that, it could be wonderful having someone to share these moments with—standing at the crib of their own baby, in their own house, their own Saturday nights. But this was an anomaly. This was Joe's way of changing her mind. Showing her he could do it and do it well, just as he did everything else. But it wouldn't last. Taking care of kids got old fast. Once the novelty was gone, he would be, too. Still, she had to give him credit.

"I...I don't know how you did it," she said.

"I told you, I didn't do anything." Modesty. One of his trademarks. One of the things that had made him successful. One of the things she loved about him.

"Yes, you did. You fed her and you put her to sleep. I tried and I couldn't. What am I going to do when my own baby won't stop crying?" A tear sprang to her eye.

Joe put his arms around her, and for a second she gave in and relaxed against him, letting all her frustration and helplessness fade away. She let him hold her, and she took strength from him. She let herself pretend he loved her and he wanted her. She let herself imagine that if she lifted her face to his, he'd kiss her, and after the children were asleep they'd tiptoe to their own room, to their king-size bed where they'd make passionate love and fall asleep in each other's arms. And if the children woke up in the night, they'd take turns getting up so the other one could sleep.

It wasn't going to happen. Even if she did marry Joe, even if he did make love to her again, he didn't love her. He never would. He would respect her, admire her, even like her. But it wasn't enough. It was weak and self-indulgent to allow herself to stay in his arms, and even worse to fantasize about something that was out of the question. He felt sorry for her. That was all, and it was her fault for letting him see the weak and uncertain side of her.

"What are you going to do?" he repeated her question softly. "You're going to marry me."

She pulled away and straightened her shoulders. She should have known. He was doing this to get his way. To convince her he'd be a great dad. He might be. But she wanted more than that. She wanted a great husband, too.

"I thought we'd been through this," she said.

"I thought you'd changed your mind."

"I haven't and I won't. But thank you for asking."

"I intend to keep asking."

"Please, Joe, you make it hard for me—"

"To say no? Then say yes."

Damn him. He was so persistent. She'd always loved that about him, too. But not when it was turned on her.

"Hey." Kyle stood in the doorway, eyeing Joe and ignoring Claudia. "You said you'd read me my *Thomas the Truck* book."

"I will," Joe said. "Would you excuse us, Claudia, or maybe you'd like to hear it, too. Sounds like a great story."

Her lips curved into a smile for the first time that day, maybe all week. She followed him to Kyle's bedroom where the little boy got into a bed that was shaped like a streamlined car and painted bright red.

"What is it about men and their cars?" she murmured. Neither of them answered her. Kyle was hanging his head over the edge of the mattress, looking for his book under his bed, and Joe was examining the other books in Kyle's bookcase.

Claudia perched on one end of the bed, and Joe sat next to Kyle while he read. Claudia's mind drifted despite her efforts to pay attention and not dream her usual daydreams. It just made reality harder to bear. One more week, she told herself. One more week and she wouldn't see him every day. After she quit, she would hardly ever see him. She wouldn't let him intrude on every aspect of her life. He wouldn't even want to. Of course, there was the doctor. She'd promised he could go with her. After all, he should go. This was his baby, too.

When Kyle's eyes finally got heavy and he agreed to let them leave his room as long as the night-light was on and his book was on his pillow, too, they went to the living room.

"Well, thanks again," she said. "You were great." She hoped he'd get the message. It's over. You can go now. But he didn't. He sat in a large easy chair by the window.

"Where did you learn how to take care of kids?" she asked.

He shrugged. "I didn't know I knew how."

"You never baby-sat, never had small kids around, cousins, anything?"

"Nope."

"Well, I don't know how to thank you."

"Don't you?" he said.

"If you mean staying on and working for you, you know I can't."

"Can't or won't?"

"Joe…"

"All right, I understand. I won't press you on that. But what about marrying me?"

She gasped. She should have known he wouldn't quit. "I thought we settled that. If that's why you came here tonight, you shouldn't have bothered. If you came to show me you could spend a Saturday night with little kids, well you did it and you did it better than I could. Much better. Is that what you want to hear? I appreciate what you've done. I really do. You never cease to amaze me, Joe.''

"Is that a yes?" he asked.

"No. You know how I feel about marriages based on…''

"Respect, trust, admiration?''

"You make it sound so easy,'' she said.

"It won't be. I know that and so do you. I don't think it's easy for anybody to be married and be a parent. But I'm willing to try.''

She stared at him. He was so reasonable, so serious, so damned rational. Too rational. She wanted passion, she wanted lust and, most of all, she wanted love. Was that so wrong? Was that so hard to find? Yes. But that didn't mean she would compromise. Not now. Not ever.

"Try? And what happens when you realize it isn't working. That your life isn't your own anymore. That your guy friends drop you because you can't go out with them on Friday nights, and you can't race your car on Saturdays because there's a dance recital or a soccer game or…''

"You think I'd walk out on you and my baby?'' he asked incredulously.

"No, I know you always keep your word. But I think you'll probably want to walk out. And that would be worse than walking. My parents never fought. There were no arguments, no shouting or slamming of doors. There was just polite silence. No affection, no love. They were just marking time, counting the days, the months, the years. They're both so much better now. I had no idea what they were really like until they split up. Now they're happy, outgoing and free at last. I see them both, independently, and I realize what they sacrificed for me, and I feel guilty. Do you want our child to feel that way?"

"No," he said.

She waited, but he didn't elaborate. He just sat there staring into space, lost in thought. She wondered if she'd finally made an impression on him. If he'd finally given up. She hoped so. It would be a huge relief. By the same token she felt a little let down. It wasn't like Joe to take defeat so easily.

"I could make some coffee," she offered, to break the silence.

"Coffee? I don't think I had dinner, did you?"

"No, but..."

"Then I'm going to order some Chinese food."

Her mouth watered. Either she was ravenous or she was unable to eat or drink anything but crackers and apple juice. This was one of the ravenous times.

Again he ordered for her. This time she didn't care and she didn't resist. She listened while he ordered enough for an army of Chinese soldiers. Mushu pork, spring rolls, General Tsu's chicken, eggplant in black bean sauce, chow mein and rice.

When he put the phone down she shook her head and smiled. "Who's going to eat all that?"

"The three of us," he said. "You and me and the baby."

The way he said it made her heart thud in her chest. You and me and the baby. It sounded like the name of a book or a song.

When the food came they sat at the kitchen table and drank tea and ate out of the cartons.

"We did this once before," he said, pausing with his chopsticks in his hand. "Maybe you don't remember, but it was a Saturday night after we'd been working all day on something."

"The Arabica project," she said. She couldn't believe he remembered that night. They'd talked and laughed for hours. Their closeness, their camaraderie had meant so much to her. She thought it had meant very little to him. He'd been dating a ballet dancer at the time. A gorgeous, tall, slender woman who'd been on a diet since she was ten years old. Joe had Claudia buy him front-row tickets every time she danced. Claudia read the reviews of her performances in the papers and clipped them for Joe. The reviewers always spoke about Giselle's "ethereal quality, her grace and her agility." Claudia had never seen her dance but she could imagine how magical it seemed.

"I remember being amazed at how much you ate," he said.

"Compared to Giselle, I suppose I did," Claudia said, realizing how stark the contrast between herself and a professional dancer must seem. She wondered how he would see her a few months from now, when she'd graduated to maternity clothes. Any woman would look slim and graceful next to her.

"You still do," he remarked, watching her take another bite of eggplant. "I like to see a woman with an appetite. I like to see you eat."

"You might not like it in a few months when I'm the size of a small blimp."

He stared at her belly, then his gaze moved to her breasts. She held her breath. Her breasts were already tender and full. Under his gaze she felt her nipples tighten and peak. She set her chopsticks down and picked up her teacup. Her face was hot. The tea slid down her throat and warmed her insides. Or was that due to something else?

Joe tore his gaze away and sat back in his chair. "I suppose I ought to go," he said.

She stood. He'd probably been sitting there wondering how to get out without seeming too abrupt.

He probably couldn't believe he'd spent Saturday night baby-sitting with his admin when he could have been out on the town.

"You must have a lot of catching up to do, now that you're back."

"I do. That's why I'm so grateful you're back to help me out."

"I meant socially. All those friends who call you. All the invitations. The parties. You know."

"Oh, those. I'm really out of the loop these days."

"I left you messages."

"I know. I haven't returned any calls. Not yet. I feel…I don't know. I was gone so long. Some of the things I used to do seem irrelevant since I got back."

Since he'd heard he was going to be a father. That's what he meant. She was sure of it. "Well, thanks for coming. I couldn't have done it without you."

"Sure you could."

"I don't think so."

"You're going to be a great mother."

"How? How do you learn how to be a parent?"

"I have no idea," he said. "Maybe it comes to you when you need it."

"I'm going to have to get a book," she said.

"Get one for me," he said.

"I don't think you need one."

She was about to see him to the door when she heard Al and Sharon come home. Damn, she didn't want Joe to meet them. She didn't want them to jump to any conclusions about Joe when she told them she was pregnant. But he did meet them. And he did turn on the charm as only he could do. He told them what great kids they had. He told them how much he'd enjoyed playing with their son and seeing their beautiful baby daughter. He didn't have to do that. Why did he? She didn't know. He'd never see them again.

"Well, we'll all have to get together one evening," Sharon said, beaming at Joe and looking back and forth from Claudia to the man who seemed to be more than a casual acquaintance of their friend Claudia. "When there are no children around," she added. "I owe you big-time Claudia." Sharon turned to Joe. "Can you believe she calls us on Thursday and *offers* to baby-sit? We didn't even ask her. That's the kind of person she is."

Claudia smiled weakly, and they finally left the house. Joe didn't say anything until they'd reached her car.

"So you volunteered to baby-sit at the last minute on Thursday, but you already knew you were baby-sitting when I asked you out for tonight."

"Yeah, well…"

"Don't apologize," he said, "for lying and hurting my feelings. After all, you thought I wouldn't find out."

"It was just a white lie, and I don't believe I hurt your feelings."

"Why, because I don't have any? Don't answer that. I understand. You see enough of me from nine to five, every day of the week. You wanted to get away from me at least on the weekend. But I don't get it, do I? I show up when I'm not wanted. Okay, I'm sorry. Sorry I'm forcing myself on you. You'll laugh when you hear I was going to insist on coming baby shopping with you."

"Yes, I would laugh. Especially when you could be out racing your car."

"I can do that anytime. But if you don't want me to come with you…"

"It's not that."

"What is it?"

She didn't want him baby shopping with her. She didn't want him baby-sitting either. It just gave her false hope that her dreams would come true when she knew they wouldn't. He had no idea what it was like to be trapped in a loveless marriage "for the sake of the child." Even when she was young she'd read between the lines, noted the awkward silences and the unexplained absences. She'd always known her parents didn't love each other. She would not bring up her child that way. Better to have a single parent than a house filled with unfulfilled promises, frustrations and disappointments. She didn't want to love him or need him, because he would never return her love and he would certainly never need her. Except around the office. After she left Callaway Coffee, and he didn't see her every day, he'd forget about her.

She'd never forget about him, but at least she wouldn't have to live with him and pretend that what she felt for him was just what he felt for her—respect, admiration and affection. She'd been hiding her love for him for three years. How much longer could she keep it up?

Joe was looking at her so strangely she was afraid she'd spoken the words out loud instead of thinking them.

"I would rather go by myself," she said.

"All right. I can respect that. As long as you're being honest. That's all I want."

"No, you don't. You want to prove you can be a father. You don't have to. I believe you. You'll probably be a better father than I'll be a mother. If tonight is any indication. But that doesn't mean I'm going to marry you."

"Fine," he said, a hint of bitterness creeping into his voice, and he opened her car door for her.

Joe stood on the curb and watched her drive

away. Damn, she was stubborn. He'd never known how obstinate she could be. In all the past three years, she'd never acted this way before. But now she had a lot at stake. Her baby. So did he. *Their* baby.

He was as determined as ever to marry her. But it was time to back off. By persisting, he risked alienating her. It was the same in business. He'd always known when to back off and give the other party time to cool down. But he'd never lost sight of his goals, either. He always got what he wanted. This time he was more determined than ever. This time there was more at stake than a simple deal. It was more than money, it was his future. His and his son's...or his daughter's.

When he got home he looked around his spotless condo. The cleaning service had been there, and there wasn't a speck of dust or a single thing out of place. It would be different with a baby. There had to be room for toys and whatever it was she was planning to buy when she went shopping.

He couldn't stay there with a baby. Even if she refused to marry him, he'd have the baby half of the time and the condo bylaws wouldn't permit it. Half of the time wasn't enough. He wanted his baby all of the time. He was going to raise this baby the way he hadn't been raised. His phone rang. It was Claudia. He felt a surge of relief mingled with hope.

"Joe, I...if you really want to come shopping with me, well, I don't mind."

"Good." This was no time to ask her why she'd changed her mind. Just accept it as a gift. "What time should I pick you up?"

"How about noon?"

"Why don't you come here? I'll get bagels and make coffee."

"You don't...all right."

"You have my address?" he asked.

She had his address, and when she came to the door the next morning, he stood back and stared as she came in.

"You look...different," he said, unable to keep from gazing at her snug blue sweater and blue jeans that hugged her hips. He'd never seen her in such casual clothes. When he'd thought about her while he was in Costa Rica, and that was often, he'd only pictured her in her office clothes. Conservative dark colors in good taste. Since then she'd filled out in a very sexy kind of way that made him uneasy.

He was surprised to realize he'd never noticed her breasts before last night. And now he couldn't stop noticing. Maybe it was the tailored suits she'd always worn that served as a kind of uniform, or maybe it was the pregnancy that had made her look like a ripe peach and downright voluptuous. Of course there was that night in his office, when she'd shed her bright red Christmas dress, but that seemed more like a dream than reality. He forced himself to concentrate on other things, so he didn't keep staring and embarrassing both of them.

"I *feel* different," she said with a smile. "I feel good today." There was color in her face today.

"I guess I shouldn't ask why you changed your mind," he said.

"No, you shouldn't," she said.

Along with her breasts there was a change in her attitude since he'd returned from Costa Rica. Surely she wasn't always this uncompromising and opinionated. She'd never been a doormat, but she'd always let him have the last word. No longer. She was the one who was calling the shots with this baby and with his plans.

He spread the bagels, cream cheese, lox and sliced tomato on the table along with a pitcher of fresh-squeezed orange juice and watched with some amusement and more than a little pleasure as she downed a glass of juice and spread cream cheese on her bagel.

"You're staring at me," she said, glancing up at him, her second bagel in her hand. "I know, I'm going to weigh two-hundred pounds, but I'm so hungry."

"I don't care if you're three-hundred pounds," he said. "I still want to marry you. Now."

She set her bagel down and glared at him.

"Sorry," he said. "I forgot. I wasn't going to mention it again. Not today, anyway."

"This is a nice place," she said after a long pause, glancing around at the pale walls, the granite countertops and the high ceilings. "But it doesn't look as if anyone lives here. Don't you have any pictures?"

"Yes, in the living room there's a copy of a Chagall."

"I mean pictures as in photographs. Of your family, maybe."

"My parents? You want to see pictures of my parents?"

"I just wondered," she said. She had no idea she had stirred up a hornet's nest.

"You asked me once why I always dumped every woman who showed interest in me beyond just dating."

"Never mind," she said. "It was none of my business."

"You told me about your parents, now I'll tell you about mine."

"No, really. It's not necessary." She didn't want to know any more about Joe than she did. She didn't want to care any more about him than she did. She wanted to believe he sprang fully hatched from an egg, dressed in a three-piece suit wearing Italian shoes and handmade shirts.

"I was a hell-raiser as a child," he said. "At least that's what they called me."

"Who called you that, your parents?" she asked, her eyes wide with surprise.

"They did, my teachers did, and so did the head-master at the boarding school where they sent me at age ten."

"That seems kind of young," she murmured. Now it was happening. She didn't want to, but she was picturing ten-year-old Joe at boarding school, alone and lonely.

"It is young, but they felt I was unmanageable. I probably was."

"But couldn't they…"

"Have tried something else less drastic? I think so. I don't know what, but… Anyway, that was the last time I lived with them on any permanent basis. They sent me to camp in the summer."

She couldn't help it, tears sprang to her eyes. She blamed it on the hormones. After all, even a Hall-mark commercial could make her tear up.

"It's not worth crying over. I didn't want to go home. I preferred camp."

"What about Christmas?" she asked.

"Oh, yes, Christmas. We went skiing at Christmas. That way I'd be in ski class all day and less of a pain.''

''But that's awful. You couldn't have been that bad,'' she said.

''Couldn't I? I wonder. What if we have a kid like that? What if you can't handle him, Claudia? Don't you see now why we have to be a unified front? Why we have to get married?''

''Is that what this was all about? Just another way of trying to convince me?'' she demanded, feeling as if she'd been taken.

''I wanted to explain why I wouldn't let anyone get close to me, especially women. I know you didn't approve when I dumped them. Oh, you sent the flowers and you wrote the notes and you fielded their calls, but I could tell by the look in your eyes, you didn't like it. Just to let you know, and this may sound like psychobabble, but it may be that deep down I'm afraid of being left. Again. So that's why I have to do the leaving.'' He couldn't tell what she thought of his self-analysis, probably not much. ''That's probably hogwash,'' he said.

''No, it's probably pretty close to the truth,'' she said thoughtfully. ''Do you think you'll ever get over it?'' she asked.

''I'd like to think I'm over it now,'' he said, ''because I want you to trust me. Anyway, I didn't mean to go into all that. I just wanted to say that you might be pregnant with a very bad boy. But no matter how bad he is, I have no intention of leaving him or you. I want you to think about it.''

''You're making it impossible for me to think about anything else,'' she said.

''Good,'' he said. ''This place is really too big for one person. Two bedrooms, two and a half baths, a study and a deck. I don't need all that space.''

She flicked a glance in his direction. He held out his hand, palm forward. ''That was merely a statement of fact. Nothing more. There are no kids allowed in the building, by the way.''

''I see.''

He could tell that she didn't see, and now was not the time to tell her he was not wedded to this condo. It had been fine when he was a swinging single, and though he might stay single, unless she relented, he had no intention of swinging again. He'd buy a house in the suburbs in a minute. Something with a big yard. If only she'd say yes. Even if she didn't, he had to have some kind of a place to take the kid on his weekends.

The thought of being a single dad made his head hurt. The thought of his kid being shuttled back and forth between houses, between parents who didn't love each other. He hated the idea. He hoped that by telling her his story, she'd realize how important it was for them to get married. He certainly didn't tell her so she'd feel sorry for him. He didn't want pity. That was why he'd underplayed his hurt and resentment and his loneliness. But it hadn't worked.

She was holding firm about not marrying him. Just because she didn't love him and he didn't love her. There was no getting around that. It was too bad, but was it really that important? Claudia was a lovable person. If he didn't love her, somebody would, someday. Somebody else in the picture? Somebody else playing his role with his kid? No, he couldn't stand that. What if it happened? He had to convince her to marry him now.

The seemingly unsolvable problem took his appetite away. He tried a few bites of a bagel while Claudia ate hers, then they left for the stores. She'd made a list of discount places like Baby World, Baby Heaven, and after visiting them they went to several department stores before she was ready to buy. As she assembled her purchases, she ticked them off her list. Crib, changing table, car seat, backpack, stroller, portable crib, bassinet, sheets, blankets… It went on for pages.

When it came to paying, he took her credit card out of her hand and replaced it with his. She protested but he insisted.

"This is a no-brainer," he said. "I know how much money you make, and you know I can afford this, so don't bother to argue because I intend to win.''

The clerk looked amused. "This is a first," he said. "Parents fighting over the bill and each wanting to pay. This is one lucky baby with two wonderful, generous parents."

One lucky baby. Two parents. The words hung in the air.

Joe avoided looking at Claudia and she fumbled with her wallet.

"Will you be taking these things with you?" the clerk asked. "Do you have a van or SUV?"

Joe almost choked. Did he look like the SUV type?

"He has a sports car," Claudia said.

"Then we'll deliver. Address?"

Joe turned to Claudia. "I have lots of storage space. Have them sent to my house."

She hesitated for a moment, then she agreed. What else could she do? He had seen her friend's apartment. It appeared to be full of people and stuff. Which bothered him. Over gooey cinnamon rolls at a shop in the mall, he brought up the subject.

"How long do you plan to live with your friend Molly?" He carefully kept his voice neutral, so as not to put her on guard. The new Claudia seemed so edgy at times, so ready to take offense.

"I don't know. As long as it works out, I guess."

"You don't mean to stay after the baby comes." This time he couldn't keep the disapproval out of his voice.

"Why not?" she asked. Her lower lip was covered with a white sugary glaze. He stared at it, seized by an urge to see if it tasted as sweet as it looked. Instead he brushed his thumb across her lips. Her eyes widened and her cheeks flushed.

"Just getting rid of some frosting," he said matter-of-factly. But he didn't feel matter-of-fact. He felt charged with some strange kind of energy. He wanted to lean across the table and kiss her, but he couldn't, not in the middle of a crowded mall. And he shouldn't, not when he knew she'd stiffen and object. He jerked his mind back to her question.

"Why not?" he repeated. "Do I have to spell it out for you? Because it's crowded. There are cats. There's smoke in the air, and it's noisy. If you don't care about yourself, think of the baby. These influences can't be good for a baby, not now, not later." She wouldn't like hearing this, but he didn't care.

"And where do you suggest I live?" she asked stiffly. "And don't say with you."

"Why not? Because it's the obvious solution, isn't it? There is no reason why you shouldn't live with me. And I mean now. You want to save money? I won't charge you rent."

"Then I won't do it."

He smothered a smile. He'd won. He wasn't sure how he'd done it, but he had. He sighed and feigned defeat. ''Oh, all right. Pay me rent if you have to. But move in now, today.''

She sucked in a sharp breath. ''No, I can't. Not today, not ever. It's a ridiculous idea.''

Chapter Five

Joe felt as if Claudia had slapped him. He should have known she'd say no. He should have known she wouldn't agree, no matter how much sense it made. But just for a minute…he'd believed she would do it.

For a rare moment he was speechless. He'd thought, he'd hoped, he'd believed she would see reason, but she hadn't.

Claudia shredded the napkin in her lap and stood up. She couldn't believe he'd suggested she move in with him. What a terrible idea that was. He was persuasive, she'd give him that, and even though she knew he was right about some things, he was dead wrong about this. True, Molly's place was not a good place for a baby nor for an expectant mother, and she couldn't stay there forever. When the baby came she'd move out and find her own place, but that was months from now.

In the meantime the situation was bearable and the price was right. Joe had persuaded her to stay in the office longer than she wanted, but moving in with him was a different matter. Imagine waking up in the morning and seeing him at the breakfast table. No, Joe didn't eat breakfast at home. He waited till he got to the office to have his coffee. Well, anyway, there he'd be, mornings and evenings. Their paths would cross no matter how large the condo was, no matter how much space he'd give her.

She couldn't take it. She wouldn't take it. He could use whatever powers he had to convince her to marry him and to work for him and to move in with him, but her sense of self-preservation would stop her from falling for any and all of his arguments.

With her mind in turmoil she walked through the mall with Joe at her side, past stores that smelled like perfumes and expensive soaps, past mannequins in dresses and men's suits, past trendy shoe shops and fancy chocolatiers. All without seeing them. Until they came to a GapKids store that featured irresistible little outfits in the window for boys and girls. She stopped and pressed her nose against the window. Someday she'd have a toddler, either a boy in shorts with a matching striped rugby shirt and sturdy shoes or a girl in pink overalls and ribbons in her hair. Her eyes misted over. How would she manage to raise this child and work at the same time? What part would Joe play in this child's life? Would he really stick to his plan of taking a role because of his own childhood? Or would his interest fade as she suspected it would when the reality set in?

He stood next to her at the window, so close she could feel the heat from his body. This was such a bad idea, shopping with him. It was a horrible idea to see him on the weekends, dressed in slacks and casual T-shirts. It was awful to have to listen to the story of his life because it made her understand him better, and she didn't want to understand him at all. It was painful. All this exposure made him seem part of her everyday life. But he wasn't. He never would be.

It also made her want what she couldn't have—a husband she could love. A husband she could count on, a father to her baby. If she couldn't get through a day of shopping, how could she even think of living under the same roof with him? She couldn't. It would be pure torture. The kind of torture that eats away at a person's self-esteem. Eventually she would fold. She'd have to leave town to get away from him or it would tear her heart in two when he realized she was in love with him. What then, would he feel so much pity for her he wouldn't be able to conceal it? She'd rather he hated her than pitied her. If she was careful, very careful, he would never know how she felt.

What was he thinking at this moment? She stole a glance in his direction. Was it possible he was just as touched as she was by the sight of the childlike models in the window? Was he just as full of questions and worries about the future? Joe Callaway, the coffee king, take-charge man, self-made millionaire, uncertain about the future? It was possible. She almost put her hand on his shoulder and told him not to worry. Not to worry if he wasn't ready to be a father. Not to worry about taking care of her or the baby. She was prepared to do both. But she didn't. She kept her arms stiffly at her sides, her hands balled into fists. Then she turned and they walked to the parking lot.

When she got back to the apartment, after an almost silent ride to her house, she got out of the car before he'd even put the brake on and hurried to her front door. She hoped none of Molly's friends would be there, especially her ever-present boyfriend. She needed time to herself and some peace and quiet.

Molly met her at the door. "Claudia," she said, her forehead wrinkled in a frown. "I have to talk to you."

Claudia had a sinking feeling in her stomach, a premonition that all was not well. "Molly," she said, concerned for her friend. "What is it? Are you okay?"

"Yes, sure. It's just, Vince is going to move in with me."

Claudia's heart fell. "Oh."

"I thought maybe you wouldn't mind leaving," Molly said. "Now that you've got a new boyfriend, you might want to have your own place, for privacy or whatever…"

"No, oh, no, Joe's not my boyfriend, he's my boss. How could you think…"

"He seems so nice," Molly said. "I wish I had a boss like that." Molly tossed a cat off the couch so she could sit down.

"He is, but…" Oh, Lord, what now? Where would she go? What would she do?

"What's going on between you two?" Molly asked. "And don't say nothing. I felt something in the air that time he came here."

Something in the air? There was tension in the air. That was all. "We're friends, sort of. Don't worry about me. I'll find another place. It's no problem." No problem? It was a terrible problem.

"Are you sure?" Molly asked, her eyes wide and anxious.

"Positive. I'll be gone by the end of the week."

''Now wait, there's no hurry.''

But there was. Claudia knew it. Even before Joe had given his negative opinion on her living situation, Claudia knew it wasn't the best place for her. Later, alone in her room, she called every friend she had, but she knew what the answer would be. She'd called them all just weeks ago when she found out she had to move. Molly was the only one who'd come through for her. The only one who had a spare bedroom.

Lying in bed that night, she knew there was only one option. The one person she couldn't, shouldn't move in with. He had invited her. Had room for her. Wanted her. Why? Because he felt guilty, and like the good person he was, he felt responsible for her.

All night she tossed and turned trying to think of an alternative. Work with Joe? Live with Joe? While being in love with Joe? She buried her head in her pillow to block the images she couldn't bear thinking about. Joe at the dinner table, Joe at the breakfast table, even though he didn't eat breakfast before he got to work. What about the weekends? Joe would be lounging about in sweatpants, bare feet and bare chest. She groaned out loud as her vivid imagination went to work.

Joe would appear in the hallway in boxer shorts. Joe would be in the living room in a bathrobe reading the paper as she tiptoed by. No, no, no.

All through the night she grabbed at different solutions, but none made any more sense than moving in with Joe, which she vowed she'd never do. Finally she got up and went to work early without breakfast, though she knew it was a no-no.

"To avoid morning sickness, always keep some food in your stomach," the nutritionist had told her. Claudia just knew she couldn't get a thing down her throat today. Not until she'd figured out what to do. It was a good thing she'd come in early. She had a lot of work to do to prepare for Joe's meeting with the board of directors of the company. The work was a welcome change from lying in bed thinking about her own problems. There was no one else in the office, no one else in the whole building. In an hour or two, working without the interruption of phones or people coming into her office, she was able to have all the papers ready for Joe when he got there.

He burst into her office looking as haggard as she felt.

"Well?" he said, looming over her desk in his suit, with his tie askew. "Are you ready?"

She jumped up from her desk and handed him a stack of file folders. "I just need to download one more thing and then…"

"I'm not talking about the meeting," he said, setting the folders on her desk. "I'm talking about your moving in with me. Are you ready or not?"

She blanched. She couldn't believe he hadn't accepted her word. On the other hand, since when had Joe Callaway ever taken no for an answer?

"No, I'm not ready to move in with you, not now, not ever," she said. This was one time he would not get his way.

"Then what are you going to do?" he asked, coming so close she could see that his eyes were bloodshot as if he hadn't slept that night. He was so close she could smell the soap he used. So close he made her knees feel weak. What was wrong with him? He didn't need a place to live. He didn't need a new job. What right did he have to look as if he'd been suffering and hadn't slept?

"I haven't decided," she said, proud of the steadiness of her voice. "I'll let you know as soon as I do."

"That's good of you," he said. "And what am I supposed to do while I'm waiting for your answer?"

"I don't know. Go to meetings. Go play handball. Go out with friends."

"Easy for you to say. You're the one who makes the decisions, who has the power to decide the fate of our child. I don't like being out of the loop," he said, his blue eyes flashing.

"You're not out of the loop," she said. She was determined to match his determination, but not his anger and frustration. By contrast she felt positively calm. So calm she was able to automatically straighten his tie. How many times had she done that before an important meeting, sometimes even brushing his jacket with a clothes brush she kept in her desk. It was all so familiar and yet so strange. Before he was just her boss. Now he was more than that. Yet less than what she wanted. "You're storing the baby stuff. You helped pick it out. You're coming to the doctor with me. Does that sound like someone who's out of the loop?"

"What about those childbirth classes?"

"Yes, fine, come to the classes if you like." If she could just keep him happy with this kind of thing, maybe he'd forget about her moving in with him.

With his tie now straight, she gave him a small smile, but when she met his gaze she saw something in his eyes she'd never seen before. Something she didn't recognize. Her smile faded. "What is it?" she said. "Is it the meeting? Are you worried about the report to the stockholders because if you are…"

"No, I'm not worried about the stockholders or the trustees or anything pertaining to Callaway Coffee," he said.

She waited for him to say what it was he was worried about, but he didn't. He just stood there staring at her, making her feel more and more uneasy. Pretty soon she tore her gaze away and glanced at her watch. He nodded, picked up the folders from her desk and left her office without another word.

The minutes dragged by. From her office she heard the men—there were currently no women on the board—arriving for the meeting. There were friendly greetings, even laughter. Then silence after they adjourned to the boardroom. Claudia wished she could be a fly on the wall. These meetings could be tense. They'd ask questions about expenses, about the budget and the price of coffee beans. They might try to put Joe on the spot, ask him to justify his plans.

She was now so hungry she went downstairs to the coffee shop and bought a cup of tea and a dough-nut to go. She'd eaten half of it when Joe called her on the intercom.

"Claudia, could you bring in the report from the Latin American consortium?"

"Of course. Right away," she said. She grabbed a copy of the report from a pile on her desk and went to the boardroom. She was anxious to get a read on the atmosphere there. There were about ten men around the long table, most of whom she knew, with Joe at one end. There was a coffee cup brim-ming with Callaway's finest in front of everyone. The atmosphere seemed convivial and the air was thick with cigar smoke. She coughed gently and handed him the report.

"You gentlemen know my assistant Claudia Madison?" Joe asked. They all murmured something polite and smiled at her.

"Your secret weapon, Callaway," one of the men said with an appreciative glance at Claudia.

Then Joe asked Claudia to explain the Blue Grotto plan. She was pleased and flattered when he told them it was her idea. She managed a few coherent sentences before the cigar smoke got to her. All of a sudden she felt a wave of nausea. She willed herself to be strong. She excused herself, but the door seemed to be miles away.

She shouldn't have eaten that doughnut. She should have left as soon as she'd delivered the papers. She should have walked out as soon as she'd smelled cigar smoke. Now it was suddenly touch-and-go whether she'd make it out of the room before disgracing herself. The faces swam before her eyes. Joe stood and watched her leave. His face was lined with concern. There were voices, there was talk, but she didn't know what they were saying.

She was almost out now, she was pushing the door open and running down the hall to the ladies' room. She was hanging her head over the toilet gagging. She'd never felt so sick in her life.

The outer door to the bathroom opened. Claudia held her breath, not wanting anyone's attention or sympathy. So far no one at Callaway Coffee knew she was pregnant but Joe. That's the way she wanted to keep it. The door to her stall burst open and strong hands circled her waist and held her. She turned her head toward him and threw up on Joe's two-hundred-dollar Italian leather shoes.

She burst into tears.

"Now," he said. "Now will you marry me?"

She couldn't tell if she was laughing or crying. She only knew she was no longer vomiting, but that she was on the border of hysteria. Only Joe would pick a time like that to press his case. Only Joe would be so single-minded. Only Joe would over-look her shame and embarrassment and home in on what was important. Only Joe would come to her aid at a time like that. If ever she'd loved him, she loved him more right that moment than she thought possible.

He pulled her up and held her gently by the el-bows. Her breathing was ragged and uneven.

"Slowly, slowly. Take a deep breath," he said, patting her on the back as if she was a baby. "Re-lax."

She nodded. Her head felt as heavy as stone. She rested it on his chest and inhaled the comforting aroma of his clean shirt. She was only vaguely aware of someone else at the bathroom door. There was a gasp of surprise and a woman's voice that said, "Sorry. I didn't know…" Then the door closed.

"You didn't answer my question," he said.

"The same question?"

"Yes."

"Then it's the same answer," she said.

"What about moving in with me?" he asked.

She was so weak and his hands that held her were so strong, she could no longer resist. "Yes, all right," she said.

He didn't gloat. He didn't grin. He just nodded. But he'd won and he knew it. Or had he?

"I'm paying rent," Claudia said, her voice muffled against his shirt. "Just so you know."

"Of course." He wiped the tears from her cheek with his handkerchief as if this was a normal occurrence, having your pregnant admin vomit on your shoes then ask her to marry you, get turned down and settle with her moving in with you as you blotted her tears with your five-dollar linen handkerchief. "I could deduct it out of your paycheck if you like. It would be more businesslike."

"Yes, that's good," she murmured. It wasn't until later she realized she wouldn't be getting a paycheck after the end of the week. "It's purely a business arrangement," she said to herself. Sure it was.

Only a few hours later, after she'd sneaked down the hall to her office, her stomach calm at last, the meeting adjourned, did she realize what a big step she'd taken. She was plagued with regrets. Regrets that she'd told Joe she'd move in with him, regrets she'd ever come back to work and regrets she'd ever told him about the baby.

She thought of all the equipment delivered to his apartment. She thought of the endless months ahead of them while they waited until the baby was born. She thought of the upcoming doctor's appointment. But mostly she thought about how she was going to keep her secret from Joe and from the world. Not the secret of the baby. That was out of the bag. The secret of her love for Joe. Far from being squelched. Far from being over. Everything he did made her love him more. Made her love harder to live with and harder to hide.

Two days later Joe had moved Claudia's clothes and books into the spare bedroom at his condo and had even persuaded Claudia to go to the health club with him. He was pleased with the progress he'd made with her, until his friend Andy approached him in the locker room.

"What ever happened with you and the woman you wanted to marry?"

"Oh, that. I'm making progress. She's here tonight working with a personal trainer, and I got her to move in with me," he said.

"That's probably better. Just live together. That way you can get out of it when you want to."

"I won't want to," Joe said. If anything, he was more convinced than ever that marriage was the only way to go.

"How's it working out?"

"So-so," he said. Actually it wasn't working out the way he thought it would. He thought they'd have more contact with each other, but Claudia went to her room right after dinner. And during dinner, which Joe insisted on providing from one of the restaurants that delivered to your door, she read a magazine.

They went to work together, but he had to let her off in front of the building, then he parked in the garage. No one had seen them together so far. But Claudia was nervous about it. She wanted to take the bus home or drive her own car. He told her that was ridiculous.

"So the romantic dinners and gifts did the trick."

"No, I had to twist her arm to get her to move in. She's one stubborn woman."

"Sounds like a match made in heaven. Because you're one stubborn guy."

"She doesn't see it that way."

"Want me to have a word with her?"

Joe shook his head. "I doubt that would do any good. I've tried everything."

"Except for the romance. I'm telling you it worked with Michelle."

"I'm telling you I tried. She turned me down."

"What about a dinner for the four of us at a restaurant. Then Michelle and I will leave early. When you're alone with her, you can pull out a diamond ring or whatever it takes."

"I'll give it another try," Joe promised. They went to the parking lot together so Andy could see Joe's new car.

Andy got into the driver's seat and examined the GPS system, turned on the audio, shifted the seat back and forth and asked how fast it could go.

"They say 150, but I don't really know yet. I'm waiting to take it down to Monterey to check it out."

"This is the kind of car I always wanted," Andy said. "Before I had kids and had to get an SUV. I envy you."

"Come with me to Monterey to the track. You can take it out and see how fast it can go."

Andy shook his head. "I can't. Every weekend is taken up—kids' soccer games, stuff around the house. Are you sure you want to get married?" he asked.

"Pretty sure," Joe said. Actually he was very sure. Although he had no intention of ever trading his pride and joy for an SUV. Andy must be exaggerating.

Joe waited impatiently in the parking lot for Claudia to come out the back door of the health club. He was glad to see her looking so well. Her skin glowed and her eyes looked bright. He put his arm around her.

She told him she'd enjoyed it. She raved about her personal trainer, Jake, until he got tired of hearing about the amazing guy who just happened to be strong, kind and helpful. Those were just a few of the adjectives she used to describe Jake.

"So, you're coming back to the club with me?"

"Of course. Twice a week. Jake understands about pregnant women. He's designed a special course for me."

"Well, that's great." Of course he was happy about it. It was his idea after all. It was something they could do together. Something they could share—him, her and Jake. He just hadn't counted on her being so attached to her trainer. There were stories about women running off with their trainers for all the reasons she'd mentioned—strong, caring, understanding, kind.... Maybe this wasn't such a good idea after all.

"Now what?" she said.

"Aren't you tired?" he asked. He'd had a good workout with Andy and lifted some weights, as well.

"Not really. If I promise not to throw up on your shoes, can we get coffee and doughnuts?"

"Is this one of those cravings I've been reading about?"

"It seems to be. I've never eaten doughnuts before, but now I love them. Don't tell Dr. Taylor."

"I'll tell her you eat nothing but raw broccoli and cod liver oil," he said with a conspiratorial wink.

Chapter Six

Joe didn't have a chance to tell Dr. Taylor anything about Claudia's cravings when they went to see her. Dr. Taylor was full of questions and information for both of them.

"I'm very very glad to see you taking an interest in this pregnancy," she said to Joe. Like he was some kind of absentee father.

He opened his mouth to tell her he hadn't been told about this pregnancy until recently or he would have been there at the first appointment, but thought better of it. He also thought about enlisting the doctor's help in persuading Claudia to marry him, though it was certain Claudia wouldn't like it and would feel they were ganging up on her. She looked a little tense today. It was partly because she was afraid someone at the office might see them leaving together or coming to work together. He didn't care if they did. He didn't care who knew about them.

After Claudia's physical exam, Dr. Taylor called them both into her office. Joe felt now was his chance to ask some questions.

"Don't you think," he said, "that kids are better off when their parents are married and share the same home?"

"Of course," the doctor said. "In a perfect world it would be that way for every child."

"But it's not a perfect world," Claudia said.

Joe shot her a sidelong glance. "We have the power to make it as perfect as possible," he said.

Claudia's eyebrows shot up in surprise. "Joe…"

"I can see you two have some decisions to make," Dr. Taylor said, shifting her gaze from Joe to Claudia.

"How long do you recommend that women work?" Joe asked next. He felt Claudia stiffen next to him.

"That depends on how they feel and what kind of work they do. I'd advise against heavy lifting or high-stress jobs like air-traffic controllers."

"Claudia is my administrative assistant. I feel like I can't get along without her."

"How does she feel?" Dr. Taylor asked.

There was a long silence. Claudia looked at the doctor, than at Joe.

"I am planning to quit at the end of the week," Claudia said.

"Do you have any plans?" the doctor asked.

"Well, I…" Claudia said.

"You may be bored just sitting at home doing nothing for seven months. But if you find your present job is too much for you…perhaps your boss here can lighten your load somehow. Shorten your hours and let you take a nap after lunch," Dr. Taylor suggested.

"She can do whatever she wants," Joe said. "Work as little or as much as she likes, just so she's around. I need her and I think she needs to feel useful."

The doctor smiled at them both, then looked at Claudia. "It sounds like an ideal situation. A boss who's looking out for your welfare, and the baby's."

Claudia didn't say anything. Joe hoped she wasn't mad at him for bringing up the subject. He couldn't tell by the look on her face.

After Claudia made an appointment for her next visit they left the office. He didn't say anything further. He knew she'd have to make her own decision, but he was heartened by the doctor's opinion. Surely Claudia would rethink her decision and see reason.

After the appointment they took the hospital tour. The doctor said there was no hurry, but Joe wanted to see the facilities, and he convinced Claudia there was no need to hurry back to the office.

First they were shown the admitting area where they'd check in. Then they visited one of the labor rooms that was painted a soothing pale yellow.

"How long will we be in here?" Joe asked the nurse who was giving the tour.

He saw Claudia give him a quizzical look. Was it because he'd said *we,* instead of *she?* He intended to be with her every step of the way.

"That depends," the nurse said. "You'll hear more about the different stages of labor from your labor coach."

Next was the delivery room. All around them were doctors in green scrubs rushing from room to room, nurses in white wheeling patients down the hall, and personnel being paged over the loud-speaker system. Joe tried to imagine being there, watching his baby being born, but it was a long way off and Claudia hardly looked pregnant.

The best part of the tour was the nursery, where they got to see the newborns. They stood at the glass window staring at the tiny babies in their cribs. He was a little sad to see that some of them cried. He wanted to pick them up one by one and tell them everything would be okay. He wondered if their baby would have black or brown hair or maybe no hair at all. Would he have a round face or a long thin face? Brown or blue eyes? He wondered what Claudia had looked like as a baby. He slanted a glance in her direction and saw her face reflected his feelings—longing, worry, sympathy and even fear. He guessed it might be fear she wouldn't be a good parent, fear something might be wrong with the baby.

He reached for her hand and gave it a reassuring squeeze. She didn't say anything. When the tour was over they went back to work.

Back at the office in the afternoon Claudia had lined up one more job candidate for Joe to interview. She was feeling desperate, knowing her self-imposed deadline of two weeks was almost upon them. That was before they'd been to the doctor's. Of course the doctor was right, Claudia couldn't find a nicer, more understanding boss than Joe. When the doctor asked her what her plans were, she realized she had none but some fuzzy thoughts about being a teacher. But that would take going back to school to get credentials and doing practice teaching before she'd ever be ready. What would she do for the next seven months? She pictured herself in Joe's immaculate condo, day after day, walking from room to room, skirting the cleaning people, looking out the window, trying to read her pregnancy manual, calling friends but not wanting to tell them she was pregnant.

Joe was the one person she could talk to. About work, about the future and the past and the baby. If only...

After the interview Joe came into her office. "I've decided," he said, "to hire Ms. Jones."

"What?" She got up from her swivel chair, then sat down again. Just when she was thinking she ought to stay, he'd hired an attractive woman with all the right background to take her place. She felt as though he'd pulled the rug out from under her feet, though there was no rug on the hardwood floor of her office.

"What's wrong?" he asked. "Isn't that what you wanted? Isn't she a good choice?"

She swallowed over a lump in her throat. "Well, yes, I'm just surprised, that's all."

"I got the idea from your doctor," he said.

Claudia racked her brain. What had the doctor said to make him hire the next candidate he saw, and an attractive redhead to boot?

"To get you an assistant. Yes, if you approve of her, I'm going to hire her to be your assistant."

Claudia was so surprised she couldn't speak for a long moment. When she did, she found she was stuttering.

"Did I... Did you... I didn't know I was staying."

"Didn't you hear what your doctor said? It's an ideal situation...you have a boss who understands your situation and who cares about you. Where else are you going to find somebody like me?" he asked with a wry smile.

Where indeed? That was the problem. There was no one else like Joe. But he didn't love her. Wasn't it better to find someone who wasn't quite perfect but who'd love her? She braced her elbow on her desk and rested her chin in the palm of her hand.

"What will we tell people? Very soon it will become obvious that I'm pregnant."

"We'll think of something," he said.

She shook her head.

"Don't worry about it," he said soothingly. "Let's take it one day at a time."

He walked around behind her desk and placed his hands on her shoulders. Then he began to massage her shoulders and neck and back with his strong hands until she felt as if her body had turned to gelatin. She heard herself making small sounds of pleasure in the back of her throat. All the tension flowed out of her body. She forgot what it was that was bothering her. All she could think of was Joe. His touch was magic, and she wanted it to go on forever.

"Claudia," he said, his voice low and rough. "Don't worry. It's not good for you and it's not good for the baby. Tell me what you want and I'll give it to you. If it's not an assistant, then whatever it is you can have it."

She didn't answer. What would he have done if she'd told him all she wanted was his love. He'd have dropped his hands to his sides and gone running from the room.

After a long moment she forced herself to sit up straight. His hands were still resting on her shoulders. She couldn't look at him. She sighed loudly.

"All right," she said. "I'll stay as long as I can. Thank you for getting me an assistant."

"You're welcome," he said. She couldn't tell what he was feeling. If he was gloating that he'd won, or if he was surprised she'd given in, or if he was simply relieved he could stop interviewing candidates for her job. He patted her head like a dog who'd done what he was supposed to do. Then he left her office.

She talked to her new assistant and found she liked her very much. The woman would have an office down the hall. She was to start on Monday and Claudia could already see some things she could do that would help her out. Those were the pluses.

On the minus side she had no idea what they were going to tell the office when it became obvious she was pregnant. Joe said he'd take care of it, but how? Another downside—she was stuck living and working with Joe until the baby was born. At that time she would finally be free. That event would put an end to both arrangements. Then she'd have to quit and take care of the baby. Then she'd have to leave his condo because of the no-children rules. Those were things Joe couldn't change. But in the meantime? That was what worried her.

Joe called her later from his office to ask if she'd like to have dinner with some friends of his, Andy and Michelle on Saturday night at a new trendy restaurant on Nob Hill. How could she say no? He'd know that she didn't have plans. That was another one of the minuses of living with him.

"They want to meet you," he said.

"They don't know, do they?" she said.

"About the baby? No. But they've heard me rave about you for years."

She could just imagine what Joe had said. *So efficient. So punctual. So hardworking.* When what she wanted him to say was *So desirable, so beautiful, so lovely.*

"Sure, that would be fine," she said.

While getting dressed on Saturday night in the spacious bedroom Joe had allocated to her, Claudia was surprised at how snug her best black dress had become. Around the bust and at the hips. She'd have to break down and buy some maternity clothes one of these days. But not until they'd decided on what to tell people. He'd said not to worry, but she did worry. She couldn't imagine a story that was believable and didn't incriminate Joe. Not only was the dress snug, but she couldn't zip it up in back.

Joe knocked on her door. "Ready?"

She opened the door. His eyes widened.

"I've never seen that dress before," he said, his eyes traveling up and down her body.

"It's not something I'd wear to work."

"No, you'd better not, or I wouldn't get any work done," he said. "It's the kind of dress that makes me want to take it off you."

She inhaled a sharp breath and tried to act as if her heart wasn't beating twice as fast. She reminded herself what had happened the last time he'd taken her dress off her. "I'm afraid it's gotten too tight for me."

He shook his head. "It must have been too loose before. I like it this way."

She blushed, surprised by the look in his eyes. For years she'd dreamed of him finding her desirable and sexy. Why now? What was it? Was it the pregnancy? It was gratifying, but it was lust, not love, she reminded herself. Still, seeing lust in Joe's eyes had only happened once before. The night of the Christmas party.

"Can you help me zip it up in back?" she asked. She turned around.

The touch of his fingers on her bare back sent shivers up her spine. He kissed the back of her neck, and now every nerve ending was tingling.

"Won't we be…aren't we late?" she asked.

"You smell so good," he murmured. "Like flowers."

"It's just the bath gel," she said. The same bath gel she'd been using for years. He'd never noticed before, or if he had, he hadn't said anything. Of course he didn't usually come this close to her. She told herself it meant nothing.

"I'll get the car," he said abruptly.

The restaurant was on a hill with a view of the city and the bay from every table.

"Do we have a reservation?" Claudia asked.

"Yes, I made it," he said. "You thought I didn't know how."

Claudia nodded. She knew he hadn't made his own restaurant reservation for at least three years because she'd done it for him. The other couple wasn't there, so they had a drink in the bar while they waited. Claudia had club soda while Joe drank a whiskey on the rocks. She felt a bit like Cinderella at the ball. Out on a Saturday night with Joe Cal-

laway in a tight black dress that drew his gaze as
well as some other gazes. So this was what it was
like. Sitting at a small table with a candle in the
middle, knocking knees with him. The hum of
voices in the background. The smell of money in
the air. She tugged at the neckline of her dress that
seemed to be just a little too low to be decent, then
she pulled at the hem of her skirt that kept creeping
up.

He reached across the table for her hand. ''Relax,'' he said.

Easy for him to say. Relax while waiting to meet
Joe's friends? Relax knowing she was pregnant with
Joe's baby and nobody knew about it but them? Relax while trying to figure out why Joe was staring
at her in that disconcerting way? Relax with her
hand in his?

''You'll like my friends,'' he said.

But she didn't get to meet them, not that night.
The maître d' came and gave Joe a note. Andy and
Michelle's little girl was sick and they couldn't
make it.

''I'm afraid you're stuck with me,'' he said, getting to his feet to follow the maître d' to their table.

So it was just the two of them at an intimate table
in the corner. White tablecloth and fresh flowers and
more candles. Just what she'd pictured in her dreams
and just what she didn't want. Though she'd always

wished it could be her who was dating Joe, instead of all those other women, now she could hardly bear to be in this position, knowing why she was there. Knowing he was on the ''date'' because he felt obligated. She thought the time would drag. She thought of making up an excuse and leaving early. But since they lived together, what would that solve? There was no escaping Joe.

That evening Joe showed her why he was in such demand as a single guy in San Francisco. Why women called him and invited him out. Why his social schedule was full. He was witty, entertaining and charming. Oh, she knew all that. But the wit and charm had never been turned on her with the force of a spotlight before. She'd never sat across a dinner table while he told stories of picking coffee beans in Costa Rica.

He told about the owner of the plantation and his family. He told her about the scenery, the volcanoes and the beaches and the sea turtles that come back to the shore every year to lay their eggs.

''They know instinctively where to go, where they'll be safe to lay their eggs,'' he said. ''As soon as they're hatched, they make a mad dash to the sea, to try to survive against horrific odds. That's why they're almost extinct. Why there are so many save-the-turtles groups, where they tag them and follow their routes.''

"Did you see them?"

"Yes. Next time I'll take you with me. And the baby. I'm never leaving you behind again. Look what happened when I did. You quit."

"I had a good reason," she said, feeling defensive.

"What was it?" he asked.

"I...I didn't think you'd be happy to hear I was pregnant," she said softly. "I was under the impression that you liked your life as it was and wouldn't want a baby around. And I didn't want you to do what you're doing."

"What I'm doing?" he said, looking perplexed. "I hired you an assistant, I let you come and go as you like and I let you vomit on my shoes. What's not to like about what I'm doing?"

"I know, I know. I'm very grateful. I just didn't want you to do it out of a sense of obligation. I wanted you to do it because you—" The words *because you love me* stuck in her throat. "Because you wanted to," she finished lamely.

"I do want to," he said. "Believe it or not I want to be a father. I don't know how to be a father, but I'm willing to try."

"You'll be better at it than I will," she said.

"Just because you had a hard time at your friends' house? Taking care of somebody else's kids has got to be different from having your own.

Doesn't it?'' he asked, running his hand through his hair.

"I hope so," she said, "because I failed miserably." Tears filled her eyes. What if she couldn't handle being a mother? What if she had to go right back to work and had to hire a nanny? Not because she needed the money—Joe would see to that—but because she was a failure at motherhood?

Joe wiped the tear from the corner of her eye. "You did not fail," he said softly. "You've never failed at anything."

She managed to give him a watery smile. "I'm sorry I didn't tell you I was pregnant," she said. "I underestimated you."

"I hope you'll never keep a secret like that from me again," he said.

She picked up her menu and used it as a barrier between them. She was afraid he'd look in her eyes and know she was hiding the biggest secret of all. She could picture his reaction as she blurted out that she was in love with him. That she'd been in love with him for years. He would turn pale, get up from the table, make some excuse and disappear. He'd accepted the baby, but he would hate to hear how she felt about him. He didn't want to be smothered with unrequited love. No one did.

After they ordered, Joe told her more about the

sea turtles. How the locals believe that the world was created on the back of a turtle.

"They're such wonderful people. So down-to-earth and hospitable. When we go we'll stay at a place right on the beach. You can see the fishermen drying their nets and bringing in the catch in the evening. We'll have dinner at one of the beach shacks where the food is simple but wonderful. You'll love it. I don't know why I didn't take you with me this last time."

"I had a lot of work to do at the office," she said. "But then I left. I left you in the lurch. I'm sorry for that. I'm not proud of myself for underestimating you. I should have told you right away. I should have known you'd do the right thing."

Her words made Joe feel hopeful. Maybe this dinner thing was working after all. Maybe he'd better try to pin her down while she was in the mood.

"If it's so right, why aren't you going to marry me?" he asked. Then he caught himself. "Never mind. I admit I was angry at first. But now I understand." He reached for her hand and held it in his. "Next time I go you won't be working for me. I don't know how I'll adjust to that. I don't know how the company can keep going."

She smiled and pulled her hand back. "You'll manage just fine. I'll have plenty of time to train someone new. Maybe my new assistant can take over for me."

Joe was worried. If she didn't work for him, and she wouldn't marry him or continue to live with him when the baby was born, when would he see her? How would he continue to be a part of their lives? The future was full of uncertainty. How long would it take him to convince her of something so obviously right for her, for him and for the baby. But now was not the time to press for an answer. He remembered Andy's advice and leaned forward across the table.

"I want to get to know you better, Claudia, I want you to know me. I want…"

He was so intent on telling her what he wanted and finding out what she wanted, he hadn't noticed the man who'd come up behind him and tapped him on the shoulder.

"I thought that was you," Dan Jenks, one of the board of directors of Callaway Coffee said. "Out on the town, huh, Joe? And this is your lovely assistant if I'm not mistaken."

Joe turned and forced a smile. He didn't want to be interrupted at that particular moment, nor any moment that evening. He wanted to focus on Claudia and he wanted her to focus on him. Whatever reason Andy chose for not showing up tonight, he was grateful.

"I didn't know you two were an item," he said, his gaze traveling from Claudia to Joe.

"We're just talking business," Claudia said quickly. Joe noticed her cheeks were tinged with pink. There was no reason for them not to be seeing each other outside of work, no reason for Claudia to be embarrassed.

"I see," Dan said with a smirk as if he'd caught them smuggling the secret recipe for Callaway Coffee to the competitors.

"Well, have fun, you two."

Joe was relieved when he left.

"Are you embarrassed to be seen with me?" he asked.

"I don't want anyone to know," she said, looking down at her napkin.

"Why? What does it matter? I don't care if the whole world knows we're an item, and I don't care if they know this is my baby."

A woman at the next table turned to look at him, and Joe realized he'd been talking too loudly. He shook his head. "I'm sorry," he said. "I'm usually more subtle. I'll try not to cause you further embarrassment in public. Now, in private, that's another matter," he added under his breath, thinking about taking her home with him, hoping she'd need help unzipping that dress, hoping she'd be receptive to something besides the usual chaste good-night be-

fore she disappeared into her bedroom. The sight of
her in that clingy black dress, the scent of her perfume, the hint of her creamy white breasts showing
at the low neckline, her long legs in those high heels
with all the straps combined to make his libido rage
and his heart pound.

All those years and he'd never really seen her,
never noticed how she bit her bottom lip when she
was worried. How she drew her eyebrows together
when she was concentrating, or how her brown eyes
darkened when she wore dark colors.

He'd thought at first she'd lost weight, but it was
just those business suits she wore to the office. Now,
tonight, in a black dress, she was all round curves.
Her skin looked like porcelain, and he wanted to
touch her so badly it hurt. He wanted to peel that
dress off her, to see her pale breasts, her slightly
rounded stomach and her bare legs. He remembered
just enough from that late-night scene in his office
to tantalize him and make him want more.

Had it worked? Was this the kind of romantic
dinner Andy recommended to change her mind? Joe
had never doubted his charms before. Not until now.
Not until it counted. He had to admit that right now
he wasn't thinking marriage, he was thinking about
making love to her. But not on the couch in his
office. This time he wanted to do it in his king-size
bed, not with stale cigar smoke in the air, but with

fresh air wafting in through the window. Not in a rush, not ripping their clothes off, but taking his time to make sure she knew how much he wanted her. This time it would have nothing to do with too much champagne. This time they would both be cold sober. This time it would mean something.

He'd seduced his share of women in the past. He knew the rules. He'd had much success. He knew the technique. Then why was he so nervous about seducing Claudia? Why so worried she would say no?

They finished dinner and left the restaurant without running into any other acquaintances. Now all he had to do was to get her home and in the right mood. They stood on the sidewalk in front of the restaurant while he waited impatiently for the valet to bring his car around. He couldn't wait another minute. He had to speak, to say something. He had to know how she felt.

"Claudia," he said softly, putting his arm around her and pulling her tightly to his side. "I want to make love to you."

Chapter Seven

The valet came before she answered. Or, he wondered, didn't she want to answer? He knew he was driving too fast in his new car, not 150 miles an hour, but above the speed limit nonetheless. She sat next to him staring out the window without saying anything. What was she thinking? Did she have any feelings for him at all? Had that first time been a fluke that she'd regretted ever since? So many questions and no answers.

By the time they got to his front door he was on fire. He couldn't wait another minute. She started down the hall to her bedroom, and he caught her hand and pulled her into his arms. She felt so good there, so right, so perfect. Surely she felt it, too.

"It's too early to go to bed yet. Alone," he said.

She looked at him with her steady dark gaze, so close yet so far away. "This is what got us into trouble the last time," she said.

"That was my fault. I should have used a condom. But we don't need one anymore."

"Why?" she asked.

"Why? Because you're pregnant," he said.

"No, why do you want to make love to me?"

"Because you're the most beautiful, desirable and sexiest woman I've ever seen. I don't know why I didn't see it before. There you were, right in the next office, and I didn't see you. Not really." He traced the line of her cheek down to her chin with his thumb.

She turned pale in the light from the overhead fixture and shook her head, slowly, sadly. "I can't do it. It would be wrong."

He felt as if his lungs had been compressed and all the air was gone. "Was it wrong the first time?" he asked.

"I couldn't help myself," she said. "But now I can. I know what I want now."

"Tell me."

She shook her head.

"Tell me you don't want to make love with me," he demanded. He kissed her then, deeply and thoroughly, until he felt her melt in his arms. Until he felt her lips respond to him. Until he was kissing her faster, deeper and more frantically and she sighed her surrender and joined him in the dance. She matched his ardor with hers, matched him kiss for kiss. The prickly spikes around the cactus plant that was Claudia had disappeared. She was soft and sweet, and he wanted her more than he'd ever wanted anyone.

He slid his hands down, caught her hips and pulled her against him.

Claudia gasped. The other time they'd been this intimate she'd been half-drunk on champagne. Tonight they had no such excuse. They both knew exactly what they were doing. Or she had known before he kissed her. Now her brain wasn't functioning quite as well.

He was an expert at kissing. He was an expert at seducing women, too. She knew that and yet here she was, in his apartment, in his arms, acting as if she was the only woman he'd ever wanted, when in reality she was just another notch in his belt. True, he probably hadn't proposed to any of the others. But he wouldn't have proposed to her, either, if she weren't pregnant. Knowing what a strong sense of honor he possessed, she was convinced he would have proposed to any woman he'd gotten pregnant. She didn't know if that made her feel better or worse.

The strength of his arousal shocked and warned her. She knew she ought to get away now, but she couldn't move. Not even when he reached for the zipper on the back of her dress and unzipped it. Her dress fell in a pool of black crepe at her ankles.

He groaned in the back of his throat and bent over to nuzzle her breasts, spilling out of her black lace demi bra.

He stopped to catch his breath. "Come to my room," he said.

"I can't," she gasped.

"Then we'll go to yours," he said.

She didn't say yes; she didn't say no. Her vocal cords were frozen and she was wracked with indecision. She turned and walked down the hall in her bikini pants and bra, leaving her dress on the floor, and he followed her. Her room, which had once been the guest room, was now completely hers, from the new curtains she'd hung at the window to the pictures on the wall and the scent of her cologne in the air. The bed was covered with a splashy flower-print comforter. It was her haven, her refuge. She was there at his invitation and she owed him a lot for giving it to her. But gratitude was a poor reason for making love. Not that she wasn't swayed. She wanted nothing more than to open her arms and her heart to him, to bask in the glow of his ardor and show him just how much she loved him. But she

couldn't. She couldn't make love to Joe here or any-
where. Not now. After the last time, she'd suffered
endless regrets. She swore she'd never go through
that again.

She turned to face him. "I'm sorry," she said,
her voice ragged and uneven. "I can't do this."

He nodded. His features were frozen. There was
a frown line between his eyebrows. "All right," he
said. "Do you mean ever or just now?"

"I don't know," she said. She wrapped her arms
around her body, but she couldn't stop shivering.

"Good night," he said stiffly. He turned and
closed the door after him. She wouldn't have blamed
him if he'd slammed it. After all, she'd led him on.
She'd let him think she wouldn't object. She'd let
him think she was just as turned on as he was. And
she was. She wanted him more than she ever had.
The better she got to know him, the more she loved
him and wanted him to make love to her. She'd
never really known him before. Certainly he'd never
known her. He still didn't. How could she expect
him to love her if he didn't know her?

She tossed her underwear on her dresser, put her
nightgown on and got into her bed. But she couldn't
sleep, and she imagined Joe couldn't, either.

The next morning on the way to work, the tension
in the car was palpable. She had to do something,
say something.

"If you're thinking of going to Monterey on the weekend to try your car, I'd like to come along."

He nodded. "Good," he said. She couldn't tell if he was angry with her, disappointed in her, disgusted with her or felt nothing at all.

She just knew she had to do something. Something to show him she was grateful to him. Not only would going with him show Joe she wanted to participate in his life, in the activity that meant the most to him, it would be a pleasant outing for her, a scenic drive down the coast, then sitting in the stands in the sunshine watching small, imported cars whiz around a track. She didn't know how dangerous it would appear, or how tense she'd feel watching him drive so fast.

But that was exactly how she felt as she sat in the stands watching the cars go by on the straightaway below. They went so fast they were a blur of black and red and white, and she could hardly tell which was Joe's. Suddenly a car spun out, crashed into the barrier and burst into flames. Claudia jumped to her feet and pressed her white knuckles against her teeth. The woman next to her told her it wasn't serious, just the equivalent of a fender-bender, but Claudia's heart was pounding, trying to see if it was Joe's car. It wasn't. Joe pulled his car over to help the driver out of his mangled car. There was a collective sigh of relief as the driver walked away, with some help from several of his friends.

"I guess I should have known it was dangerous when I saw you put that helmet on," she said when she went to meet Joe at the snack bar at lunchtime.

"No one was hurt," he assured her.

"What about that car?"

"Well, yes. It's pretty badly smashed up. But Max is fine. Just a few scratches."

She glanced at his sweaty brow, his face smudged with black grease, and noted the gleam in his eyes. "You love this, don't you?" she asked. "Is it because it's dangerous?"

"It's the speed," he said. "It's not that dangerous. Driving a car like this, going one-fifty on the straightaway, feeling how it responds, how it holds the road so well, it's incredible, fantastic. It corners as if it's on rails. You have no idea." He had a faraway look in his eyes she'd never seen before. "I feel like the car and I are one unit. I wish you could feel it. I wish I could take you with me."

She felt a half smile tug at the corner of her mouth. She'd seen yet another side of Joe Callaway. "No, thanks," she said. "I'll take your word for it."

"I thought it would be good, but it was unbelievable *how* good it was," he continued. Then, looking at her carefully, he said, "Are you tired? Do you want to go home?"

"No, of course not," she said. Even if she were tired, she would never let him know and spoil his day.

Fortunately, the afternoon passed without any incidents, no more accidents, no crashes. Claudia struck up a conversation with the woman next to her, who asked if Joe was Claudia's husband.

"No," Claudia said, "just a friend."

"The way he keeps looking up here at you," the woman, who had introduced herself as Amy, said. "I wondered."

"He's probably afraid I'll get bored and leave," Claudia said lightly.

"You must be a good friend to spend your Saturday this way."

"I wanted to see what it was all about. What the attraction was. And I owe it to him. He spent last weekend with me, doing my thing."

"Sounds like a good arrangement."

It was a good arrangement, too good to mess up with love or marriage or, even worse, with sex. Claudia was more certain than ever she'd done the right thing in turning Joe down when he'd wanted to make love the other night. She'd been frustrated, uncertain, sleepless and on edge, but she had no regrets. And Joe seemed to be his normal self. He hadn't asked her to marry him for days and he hadn't undressed her, except with his eyes, since Saturday night.

She was feeling so good about their new relationship that she agreed to go to the patron's gala night at the zoo with Joe. It was the kind of charity event he usually went to with whoever he was currently seeing, and Claudia was worried his friends would be there and wonder who in the world she was. She certainly didn't look like his other dates. No styled hair, no scarlet fingernails, no designer clothes.

The invitation said "cocktail attire." She had nothing that qualified, and if she did, it wouldn't fit anymore. Joe told her to take the afternoon off and go shopping. He tried to give her his credit card, but she refused.

"People will think I'm a kept woman," she said, standing in front of his desk in his office.

"How do you mean?" he asked, looking puzzled. "You're renting a room in my apartment. We don't have sex. That doesn't sound like a kept woman to me."

"Shhh," she cautioned, looking over her shoulder nervously.

Joe grinned, obviously enjoying her discomfort. She felt her face turn scarlet.

"You'll have to clue me in. I'm in the dark here. What is a kept woman?" he asked, his face a mask of innocence.

She gave a sigh of exasperation. "Me, explain something like that to you?" she asked. "You know perfectly well what they are. And I have no intention of letting anyone think I'm one."

"There's no danger of that," he said, "unless you decide to sleep with me. Even then you could still pay rent and then…"

"Joe, please…" she said, glaring at him.

Joe was still smiling after she'd stormed out the door on her shopping trip. He loved to tease her, to watch her cheeks turn pink and her eyes blaze. Every day he tried to say something she could find mildly offensive. Just to see her react. He didn't think he'd ever get tired of watching her catch her breath, then come up with some response to his teasing. He thought she enjoyed their bantering, too, but he wasn't sure. At least she'd agreed to attend this gala he had to go to as a patron of the zoo.

Every day he noticed a small change in her body. He looked forward to seeing her stomach grow rounder and her breasts get bigger. No matter what she wore these days, she looked sexy in it. Her hair shone with new highlights and her face glowed. She was beautiful. She might have been beautiful before, but he'd never noticed. He hoped the dress she bought would accentuate her new body.

He wasn't disappointed. She came into the living room in a stunning dark burgundy dress that was simple but the way it was draped across her body made her look elegant. The color made her skin look like alabaster, brought out red glints in her hair and made Joe feel as if he'd just run up a flight of stairs.

His heart beat a tattoo in his chest. His lungs felt as if they might burst. He took a step back to get a good look at the vision that was Claudia. He was not only breathless, he was speechless. His formerly prim and proper admin had turned into a showstopper. She noticed the look on his face and she smiled at him. A smile that said, I'm proud to be me. She turned around and let him see the back of the almost-backless dress.

''Well,'' he said at last when he'd caught his breath. ''You look beautiful.''

''So do you,'' she said, straightening his black tie.

He leaned forward and kissed her forehead. It took all the willpower he had to keep from putting his arms around her and kissing her until she gave in and kissed him back. And maybe more.

''Let's go,'' he said. While he still had his libido in check. Before he made a fool of himself. Again.

It was dusk at the zoo. Well-dressed couples were wandering around from the gorilla pit to the lion's den with glasses of champagne in their hands. Occasionally he ran into someone he knew and he introduced them to Claudia. Invariably they'd give her a curious and admiring look and he would take her arm and they'd move along. He didn't want to share her with anyone tonight.

They paused, with their arms resting on the iron fence, to watch the Asian elephants behind their enclosure.

"We patrons are encouraged to adopt one of the animals," he said. "I picked up a brochure with a list of adoptees. Tinkerbell here is available."

"Really?" Claudia said. "I'm not sure how we'd fit her into your condo."

"That could be a problem," he admitted, "but as you can see, she may be large, but she's also graceful and dignified. I can't have kids in my building, so I'll be moving in the next seven months, anyway. I want something with a backyard. Something big enough for an elephant. If we decide on the elephant."

Claudia slanted a glance in his direction. He expected a reaction from her, perhaps reminding him that this baby of theirs would only be spending every other weekend with him and didn't need a yard. But she kept quiet about that. He didn't want to argue tonight and maybe she didn't, either.

"Big enough for an elephant?" she asked.

"Why not?" he asked. "An elephant, a swing set, monkey bars and a playhouse."

She turned her head but he thought he saw a hint

of tears in her eyes. Not tears of sadness, he hoped. That's not why he'd said what he said.

"I'm not going to press you, Claudia," he said. "But I haven't given up hope. Maybe I'll still be asking you at Jacinda's graduation, but I won't give up."

"Who?"

"Our daughter. Why, what do you want to name her?"

"How about Tinkerbell?" Claudia asked.

"Won't that be confusing, having a daughter and an elephant with the same name? How would we ever know who we were talking about?" he asked. "Or who would come when we called her name?"

She laughed and he rested his arm lightly on her bare shoulders. She slanted another glance at him, and her smile faded. This time she didn't look away. This time he held her serious gaze for a long moment and something passed between them that scared the hell out of him. He felt something he'd never felt before. He didn't know what it was, and he was half-afraid to find out.

"Maybe we'd better go see the otters," he said, deliberately breaking the spell. "They're available, too."

"And they're smaller," she said as they walked toward the Otter River display hand in hand.

"Ohh, they're so cute," she said watching the

little furry animals lie on their backs and swim under the waterfall.

"Cute, yes, but we'd have to provide the climbing logs, the pool and the river. We'd better check out the gorillas before we decide."

Mkubwa was the gorilla who was up for adoption. Their brochure explained he was the patriarch of the gorilla family group, a western-lowland gorilla, father of three.

"Father of three," Joe said. "He might be able to give me some tips. Look at the way he walks around, beating his chest. He's in charge and they all know it. I think we could use a gorilla around the house, don't you?"

"In the house?" she asked.

"All right, outside the house. We'll get some rocks and plant some tall grass and some trees and leave him outside for the kids to play with. Oh, wait a minute. We don't get the real animal," he said, thumbing through the brochure. "All we get is a plush toy gorilla and a photo of our adopted animal."

"Same with the otter?" she asked.

"A plush otter and a photo. Same with Tony, the Siberian tiger, and Geraldine, the giraffe. Our adopted animal stays here at the zoo, but with the money we give, he or she gets enrichment toys, exercise devices and special treats. I think we ought to go for it.'' He stuffed the brochure in his pocket. ''Now what do you think? What do you think Joe, Jr., would like best, a stuffed tiger or an elephant or an otter?''

''Joe, Jr.? Where did that come from?'' she asked.

''Can you think of a better name for a boy?'' he asked.

''I like Mkubwa,'' she said. ''It means strength and power.''

''Mkubwa, it is,'' he said. ''I hope we learn how to pronounce it. And if it's a girl?''

''How about Porsche?''

''Portia?''

''Porsche like your car.''

The tour of the zoo was followed by the patrons' dinner under a tent, followed by the Night Owl's Ball on a specially constructed dance floor. Joe knew many of the people at the gala. This was the society he'd dallied in before he went to Costa Rica and before he learned he was going to be a father.

Several women came up to him and kissed him on the cheek and said they hadn't seen him for a long time. They glanced curiously at Claudia. He introduced her to them and wondered how he'd ever dated that kind of woman when Claudia had been around. He couldn't remember what he'd thought of Claudia then. He knew he'd depended on her. But he was ashamed to realize how much he'd taken her for granted. How little he'd appreciated her before. How surprised he was to find out she was sexy and seductive without even trying. She made all the other women there tonight look pale and uninteresting.

All he could think of was holding Claudia close while the music played. His heart was thudding before the musicians had even tuned up. He was afraid she'd say no, plead fatigue, but she went with him willingly and he put his arms around her. He prayed for slow music and he got it. He prayed she'd put her head on his shoulder and she did. He inhaled the fragrance from her hair and her skin, and he thought life didn't get much better than that. He could feel her heart beating beneath the swell of her breast, and he wanted to hold her like this forever.

He told himself he wouldn't spoil the evening by trying to seduce her. With other women it usually worked. Claudia was not other women. She was her own person. He respected her and he admired her and he wanted her. He thought she felt the same about him. He saw desire in her eyes that night, but he also saw she wasn't going to give in to her feelings.

Lucky for him he didn't love her, because he was sure she didn't love him and that would complicate everything. He remembered her words, ''You don't love me and I don't love you.'' Love was vastly overrated in his opinion.

A marriage based on respect and admiration with a healthy amount of lust mixed in? What was wrong with that? Plenty, according to Claudia. Maybe it would take years to convince her. Maybe their child would be in college before she gave in. But that would mean they'd only have one, unless…

''What do you think about raising an only child?'' he asked her in the car on the way home.

''I didn't enjoy being one, I know that. But then, I'm not raising my child under the same circumstances my parents raised me,'' she said.

He stiffened. He shouldn't have brought it up. They were back to square one.

''But ideally,'' he said, keeping his tone light, trying to capture the mood that had prevailed through the evening until now. ''How many kids do you want?''

''I don't know. Two or three.''

''Three? Three is no good. There's always an odd man out. I think we should have four.''

Claudia didn't say anything. Maybe she didn't want to spoil the mood by arguing, either. Maybe she didn't want to have any more kids with him at all. Maybe she wanted to marry someone else, someone she could love. Maybe she wanted to feel more than respect and admiration and lust. He had to know.

"What do you want, Claudia?" he asked as they went up in the elevator to his apartment.

"I don't care, the otter or the elephant or—"

"No, I mean really, what do you want out of life?"

"What everyone wants," she said, and she left him to go to her room, her cryptic words hanging in the air.

"'What everyone wants,'" he muttered to himself as he unbuttoned his dress shirt and tossed the cuff links on his dresser. "What's that supposed to mean?"

Chapter Eight

He'd barely gotten into bed when his phone rang.

"Joe? This is Ben. Sorry to call so late, but we just got word there's been a forest fire in East Africa, wiped out most of our crop of Arabica there. Thought you should know."

Joe bounded out of bed as if he'd been shot out of a cannon. "That sounds bad," he said. "I'll get on it right away. We needed that crop to meet our demand. Where are you?"

"I'm in London at the trade show. Everyone wants Callaway Coffee. That's the good news."

"The bad news is that we won't have enough to go around," Joe said, tugging his jeans on with one hand and holding the phone with the other. "We'll lose customers. They'll go to our competitors. Don't worry. I'll think of something. And try not to let the word out.''

When Joe hung up he put on a T-shirt and shoes, went to Claudia's room and knocked softly on the door.

"Bad news," he said when she opened the door. For a moment he almost forgot what the bad news was. Seeing Claudia in her long white nightgown and bare feet caused him to rock back on his heels. In the light from her bedside lamp he could see her body outlined beneath the cotton fabric. He forced his gaze away from her body. "Our coffee crop in East Africa has been wiped out by a forest fire."

"Oh, no. What are we going to do?" she asked. Not what are *you* going to do, but what are *we* going to do. How like her to assume her part in whatever had to be done. She was the best partner he could ever have or want.

"I don't know. I just wanted to tell you I'm going to the office."

"I'll come with you. We'll start calling the other suppliers."

"It might be too late. All the coffee might be bought up by our competitors."

"We have to try," she said. "Just give me a minute to get dressed."

"Are you sure you want to come?"

She didn't even answer. She didn't need to. She knew he would need her. He knew she would know how to contact the other coffee farms. She knew how much he depended on her. How could she imagine that someone could replace her? How could she think he could get along without her?

A few minutes later she joined him in the living room, dressed in sweatpants and a baggy sweatshirt. They drove to the office, let themselves into the dark and silent building with a master key and went up to the twentieth floor.

They turned on the computers, spread files all over his office and got on the phones. Their fears were well founded. Everyone in the coffee business was out looking for a replacement for the burned coffee beans. They had to be a certain kind, they had to come from certain countries and the supply was short this year and the prices were high.

But Claudia worked her magic. After making call after call, she finally found a plantation owner in an obscure corner of the world who was willing to sell to them at a decent price. After she hung up, Claudia raised her fist in the air and shouted the good news to Joe who was down the hall. He came running to her office, caught her around the waist and lifted her in the air. When she landed on her feet he kissed her.

They stood in her office in each other's arms,

looking at each other, their delight in their success a palpable presence in the air.

"You're wonderful," he said.

"No, you're wonderful," she said. "You found the names and addresses."

"You made the calls," he said. "You're the one they can't say no to."

"You could have done it," she said modestly.

He shook his head. "No way," he said. "You're amazing."

She blushed, and then she yawned.

"Go lie down on the couch in my office," he said. "It's three o'clock. I'll send the confirmation numbers and our bank draft. Then I'll call Ben in London to tell him we can meet all the orders he's taking."

"I can help you," she said.

"You're exhausted," he said. "Now go."

She gave him a sleepy smile and went to his office. It took Joe another hour to clean up the operation, to straighten out the details, and then he went to his office to get her. She was curled up on his leather couch, her hair a tangle on the throw pillow, her face flushed. He stood for a long moment looking down at her. He felt a surge of protectiveness, like the lion at the zoo, watching his mate sleep. He hoped he hadn't made her work too hard. She needed her sleep. He reached down and picked her up. She stirred and murmured something. He carried her out of the office in his arms and back down in the elevator. Despite her added weight, despite her pregnancy, she seemed light, and fitted into his arms, her breasts pressed against his chest, her head nestled in the crook of his neck.

He managed to get her into the front seat of the car and they drove through the sleeping city to his apartment. He glanced at her from time to time, wondering what he would do without her. Knowing he couldn't get along without her at the office. Hell, he'd always known that. Now it was worse. He couldn't get along without her in his life. How was he going to convince her she couldn't get along without him?

She finally woke up when he pulled into his parking space in the garage.

"What happened?" she asked, wiping the sleep from her eyes.

"We just averted a catastrophe," he said. "You and I."

"Then I fell asleep," she said. "I was dreaming about a fire."

"That was no dream," he said. "There was a fire. But thank God no one was hurt."

When they got to his apartment, Claudia was on her feet and wide awake. She had some questions about the whole operation, about the replacement coffee beans, and then she offered to make something to eat.

"I'm ravenous," she said. She went to the kitchen and opened the refrigerator. Before she'd moved in, Joe had nothing in there but a bottle of champagne and a six-pack of imported beer. She'd stocked it modestly, though Joe didn't want her to cook anything major. She had to have things for snacks, considering her appetite.

"Would you like a grilled cheese sandwich?" she asked him, taking a loaf of bread from the freezer. "That's what I'm having."

"Aren't you tired?" he asked. "Don't you want to go back to bed?"

"I slept," she reminded him. "You're the one who needs the sleep." His eyelids looked heavy, but he had a pleased expression on his face. He'd done a good night's work and he knew it. She, too, was proud of what they'd accomplished.

"It was just like old times tonight," she said. "Working together on a big project." She sliced the cheese for the sandwich and brought out a jar of pickles. Though she almost always craved doughnuts, she also enjoyed the tartness of the pickles.

"Aren't you glad you didn't quit?" he asked.

"Yes," she said. "Except…"

"You're still worried about how we'll explain your condition to the office."

Sometimes he surprised her by the way he read her mind. Was she that transparent, or was that an obvious question. Of course she was worried. Joe said he didn't care if the whole world knew about his baby, but she did. He didn't realize all the questions that would follow such an announcement. What would he do, put a notice on the bulletin board in the staff room? Or would he call a meeting? Come in with cigars for everyone, albeit a bit prematurely? Or would he leak it by telling one person, perhaps Angela, and counting on her to spread the word, which she'd be happy to do.

"Well, yes," she said. "You don't realize what kind of questions people will ask, or if they don't, they'll at least think them."

"For example?" he asked, straddling a kitchen chair while she put their sandwiches under the broiler. He was grinning at her as if it was a big joke.

"I'm serious, Joe," she said.

"So am I," he said. "Go on, give me the kind of question you're afraid of."

She was stumped. She realized that Joe was prepared to handle anything that came his way. She pressed her lips together, concentrating on toasting the bread as well as coming up with something to stump him.

"Okay, here's one," she said. "So, tell me, Joe, what are your plans?"

"Come on, Claudia, you can do better than that. The answer is, My plans are to marry Claudia, move to the suburbs and live happily ever after."

She nodded grimly. She'd walked right into that one.

"What about Claudia," she said, "is she going to keep working?"

"If she wants to," he said. "She can do whatever she wants."

She sighed loudly and put the two sandwiches on the table. Then she sat down across from him and ate hungrily. Maybe after she got some food in her stomach, some protein to her brain, she'd be able to make him see that his plan wouldn't work.

"'When is the baby due?' they might ask," she said.

"September," he said. "Nine months after we made love in my office after the Christmas party."

Claudia set her sandwich down. "You wouldn't," she said. Her face was on fire. He knew exactly what to say to make her blush. He even enjoyed seeing her get embarrassed. Of course he was joking, but hearing the words spoken out loud, even in the privacy of his kitchen, made her feel the shock all over again. The shock of realizing she was pregnant, the shock of his confronting her in the elevator, the moment when he'd guessed and forced her to confess. That was when she realized she was wrong to ever doubt he'd do the right thing and offer to marry her.

If only she knew if marrying him was the right thing for her to do. She'd been so sure. Now she sometimes wondered if she was asking too much. She had his respect and admiration. Why did she need his love, too?

The answer was that she loved him. The answer was that someday he'd find out. He was too smart, too perceptive to live with her and not know. That would be the day she'd be sorry she gave in. That would be the day she'd see pity in his eyes and hear it in his voice. No, she'd made the right decision and she was going to stick to it. When she finished her cheese sandwich she went back to bed and slept until noon.

Despite Joe's cavalier attitude, he was worried about the situation. The truth was, he had no plan other than to convince Claudia to marry him. As far as he was concerned it was the answer to all the questions. Obviously, it would solve the problem of the baby's not having two responsible parents under the same roof. And parenthetically it would answer Claudia's concern about what people would think.

He had no problem telling the whole world that he and Claudia had gotten married and were expecting a baby. "Spur of the moment decision," he would say. "Honeymoon baby," he would explain if they pressed him for details. "And we're very happy about it."

If they asked when it all happened he could be vague. "Christmas," he would say. They would understand. It was such a romantic time of year. A time to fall in love and get married. No one needed to know they weren't in love. Love was something else entirely. He wasn't sure exactly what or how it felt to be in love, but it would probably be accompanied by a roll of drums, a feeling of free-falling in space, a wish to spend the rest of your life with the other person, a sense of loss when she wasn't there. That and a healthy dose of lust along with respect, admiration, and so much more…. But that was how he felt about Claudia. Was that love?

He stood at the window of his office looking down at the traffic on the street below, wondering if he'd missed it. What if he'd fallen in love and didn't even know it? He ticked off the symptoms: wanting to make love to her, thinking about her all the time, wanting to have more children with her, to share his life with her.

He turned and looked at his leather couch, wondering if he'd fallen in love with her right there and hadn't even known it happened. If so, was it the night of the Christmas party or was it just the other night when she'd fallen asleep there? Or did it happen so gradually he'd never heard the drums or felt as if he was falling through space? Whatever, whenever it was, it didn't matter. She didn't love him and she wouldn't marry him. She'd be shocked to hear that he was in love with her. Almost as shocked as he was now that he knew what had happened. What could he possibly do that he hadn't thought of, that he hadn't already done, to convince her to marry him? Because if he didn't…he couldn't stand it. He needed her. He wanted her. He loved her.

The answer hit him one morning after a cup of dark espresso. He told the receptionist he'd be out for a while and to hold his calls. He didn't tell Claudia or anyone else. There'd be time for that later.

Claudia was in her office on the phone with her friend Sharon.

"Are you still seeing the man we met?" Sharon asked.

"Joe?" Claudia asked innocently. Did she see him? She saw him night and day, at home and at the office. "I do see him," she admitted, "but it's nothing romantic." She hoped she wouldn't be struck by lightning for lying. She wished it wasn't anything romantic. She wished she could say he was only her boss, but then how to explain why they lived together? Soon she'd have to tell her friends she was pregnant, and of course they'd assume Joe was the father. She wouldn't be able to deny it.

"Al and I thought he was just great. Perfect for you. We both noticed the way he was looking at you."

"You did?" Claudia hadn't noticed the way he was looking at her, except when she was eating everything in sight.

"And Kyle couldn't stop talking about him the next day. He must have a real way with kids."

"He does," Claudia said. And I don't.

"So how about you two joining us for dinner one night? We owe you big-time for baby-sitting."

"No, you don't, not at all," Claudia protested. "We enjoyed it. It was a real eye-opener."

"All right, we don't owe you," Sharon said. "Let's get together, anyway. Get out your calendar."

Reluctantly Claudia made a tentative date for the next Saturday night. "I'll have to check with Joe and get back to you," she said.

When she hung up she went to Joe's office and was surprised to find him gone and to hear from the receptionist he'd left without telling her or anybody where he was going. Not that he needed to. Not that she was his guardian or anything. It was just that he usually did. She called him on his cell phone, but he didn't answer. She wanted to see if there was anything he needed her to do while he was out. She left him a message. Nothing serious, she just had a quick question for him. He didn't call her back. They often went out to lunch together. Today she ate her sack lunch alone in the park. The same park where Joe had found her and made her confess. She missed him. How could that be? She'd just seen him that morning when they came to work together. She was getting soft. She was getting weak. Just when she needed to be strong.

She went back to the office, and an hour later she got a call from the hospital, the same hospital where they'd gone for their tour. The same hospital where their baby was going to be born.

"Ms. Madison? We've just admitted a Mr. Joe Callaway to St. Vincent's Hospital. He has you down as his next of kin, is that correct?"

Claudia gripped the phone with white-knuckled fingers and sat on the edge of her chair. "No, I mean yes. What is it? What's happened? Is he all right?"

"He's been in a car accident," the woman said.

Oh, Lord, going 150 and he'd smashed his car into a guard rail. She could see it now. She could hear the squeal of the brakes and smell the burning rubber, she could see the blood gushing from his forehead. She pressed a hand to her chest.

"Is he all right?" she demanded, her heart in her throat. Of course he wasn't all right. He wouldn't be in the hospital if he was all right. "Tell me," she said, "tell me how bad it is."

"He has a concussion and a broken arm," she said.

"I'll be right there," she said, and slammed down the phone. She hardly knew how she got out of the office, how she found a taxi on the crowded street, how she managed to blurt the name of the hospital to the driver, but she did.

Once inside the big, cold, stone structure on the west side of the city, she found her way to the medical wing, but had a hard time getting past the nurse at the station.

"I'm here to see Joe Callaway."

The nurse studied a chart in front of her, then looked up at Claudia. "He's only allowed to see family members during visiting hours. Three to five."

"You don't understand. I am family. I'm his…fiancée."

Claudia covered her left hand with her right just in case the nurse was checking her out for an engagement ring. After a long moment the nurse finally nodded. "All right, but only five minutes. He's drifting in and out of consciousness."

"Will he be all right?" Claudia asked, gripping the counter with her fingers.

The nurse shrugged. ''You'll have to ask the doctor.''

The room was in semidarkness, the shades were down. Dim light came from a small fixture on the wall. There were tubes hooked to Joe's wrist attached to an IV. His head was wrapped in white gauze. His face was almost as pale as the bandage.

Claudia sat in a chair at his bedside, her knees so weak she couldn't stand.

''Joe,'' she whispered.

His eyes fluttered open just slightly. He turned his head and met her gaze for just a second then closed his eyes again. Even so, she felt a surge of relief to see a sign of life. She reached for his hand and held it gently.

''How are you?'' she asked. What a stupid question. He looked awful.

His lips moved but no sound came out.

''It's okay, don't try to talk. I'm here. I won't leave.'' Let them try to make her leave after five minutes. Let them try to make her adhere to visiting hours. She sat there holding his hand and talking to him about everything and nothing and watching him. When a doctor in a white lab coat came in, he looked surprised to see her.

''I'm Dr. Allas,'' he said.

''I'm Claudia Madison, Joe's…fiancée.''

''Ah,'' he said. ''His next of kin.''

Claudia steeled herself for another lie. "Yes. Please tell me what happened and how he is."

"What happened?" The doctor consulted his chart. "Automobile accident. A rollover. Car destroyed."

Claudia gasped. Joe's car being destroyed was probably worse for him than having a concussion.

"He's actually very lucky. To come out of it with only a concussion and a broken arm. Yes, I'd say your fiancé is one lucky man." He smiled at her. "In more ways than one."

Claudia blushed at the compliment. She hoped Joe wasn't conscious to hear she'd claimed to be his fiancée. But there was no way they were going to keep her out of the room or out of the loop. No matter how many lies she had to tell.

"When will he be well enough to come home?" she asked.

"That depends. Will there be someone there to take care of him?"

"Yes, of course. Me."

The doctor took Joe's pulse, listened to his heart with his stethoscope and checked his eyes and ears with a small instrument. Then he turned to Claudia.

"He's actually doing quite well. I'd say by tomorrow he could possibly leave. But he has to have complete rest, no work, nothing."

Claudia glanced at Joe, wondering if any of this registered with him.

"He's kind of a workaholic," she explained. "He's not going to like hearing that."

"Like it or not, those are the rules," the doctor said. Then he shook her hand and said he'd tell the nurse that Claudia should be allowed to stay in the room regardless of visiting hours.

Claudia thanked him and settled into her chair, waiting for Joe to wake up. Waiting to say what she had to say, what she should have said long ago.

Chapter Nine

Joe was having a bad dream. One of those frustrating dreams where you can't say what you want to say or do what you know you have to do. In this case he wanted to speak. He wanted desperately to ask questions, of someone, anyone. He wanted to ask what had happened after he went around the corner on two wheels. He thought Claudia was there in the room. He dreamed she was holding his hand, and he even imagined he heard her say she was his fiancée, but that was obviously part of the dream.

He knew it felt like an anvil was beating out a rhythm in his head. He knew he hurt all over. He knew he couldn't move. It might have been hours or maybe days later when he came out of his dream.

He turned his head and wished he hadn't. His head felt as if it weighed about two hundred pounds and hurt like hell. Through a haze he saw Claudia in the chair next to his bed. Her head was tilted to one side and her eyes were closed. He tried to speak but he couldn't. Instead a strange, garbled sound came from his throat.

Claudia's eyes flew open and she leaned forward.

"Joe," she said. "How are you?"

"What happened?" he whispered. "Where am I?"

"You were in a car accident. You're in the hospital."

"Am I...?" He couldn't say any more. But fortunately she knew what he wanted to know. Somehow she'd always known what he wanted before he did.

"You're going to be fine," she said with a smile. "You had a concussion and you've got a broken arm. Of course, you can't do much but just rest and get well."

"I want to go home," he said.

She nodded. "Maybe tomorrow. But you can't go back to work. Not for a while."

He frowned. It was all coming back to him, the business, the orders, the suppliers, the meetings.

"Don't worry. I'll handle it," she said.

She could handle it. She could do it all. But he

thought she was going to quit, or was that just part of the nightmare?

"What about…"

"Your car? I don't know. I'll find out for you."

Just then a stern-faced nurse came in and ordered Claudia out. She said she had to bathe him and change his dressings. Claudia said she'd be back, but he was worried. Why would she stay in the hospital with him when she didn't have to? Shouldn't she be at work?

Besides the bath and the change of dressing, the nurse gave him some little pills to take, and he fell asleep again. He tried to stay awake. He wanted to see Claudia, but his eyes were too heavy and it was too great an effort to open them. He thought she was there. He thought he smelled her perfume, he thought he felt her hand on his, but that could have been part of a dream.

He wanted so desperately to talk to her. He had something to say. Something so important it couldn't wait. The only thing was, he couldn't remember what it was.

The next day when they woke him up to check his vital signs and give him his medicine, the blinds were up and he could see the outline of the Golden Gate Bridge from the window.

The nurse was cheerful, talking nonstop about the

weather and the chances that the basketball team would go to the tournament this year.

"Your fiancée will be by to pick you up around noon."

His fiancée. If only she was. Why noon? Why not now? He wanted to leave. He wanted to go home. He wanted to see Claudia.

"Seems like a nice girl," the nurse said. "When's the wedding?"

He cleared his throat. He wasn't sure he could speak. Even if he could, he didn't know the answer. "Uh…"

"Never mind. Save your strength," she said briskly.

Claudia came and then went away. They got him dressed in clothes Claudia had brought for him and gave him a lot of medicine and instructions, then they wheeled him out to the patient pickup area where she was waiting with her car.

On the way home he lay back in the passenger seat and closed his eyes. She parked in his underground garage, and he leaned on her in the elevator that took them up to his apartment.

She helped him out of his clothes and into a pair of pajamas he didn't know he owned and into his bed. She stood at the foot of his bed looking at him.

"You don't need to wait on me," he said. He

hated being dependent on her. Hated to think she had to take care of him.

"I think I can handle it for a few days," she said. "By then you'll be feeling a lot better."

"I'm better now."

She smiled. "I know. When I first saw you I thought…well, you've come a long way in two days. The good news is you weren't hurt badly."

"Claudia," he said, "I have something to tell you. You may not want to hear it, but I have to tell you."

"Me, too," she said. "I have something to tell you that you aren't going to like."

"This isn't easy," he said. Maybe he should wait until he was well. Maybe he should wait a few weeks. But he couldn't. He had to tell her now and see her reaction. He'd know right away how she felt. He expected her to be shocked, maybe even feel sorry for him.

"This is going to come as a surprise to you. Hell, it came as a surprise to me. I'm in love with you," he blurted out.

Her mouth fell open. She gripped his bedpost and stared at him.

"Joe," she said. "You're delirious. You're still under the influence of the pain medication. You don't know what you're saying. You said you were in love with me."

"I know. Please don't let it upset you. I know how you feel. You don't love me and you don't want to marry me. But I had to tell you. I couldn't keep it bottled up anymore."

"When…how…" She sat on the edge of his bed, looking stunned.

"I don't know when or how. I don't know if it was that night at the zoo or the day you came back to get your cactus. I just know that I've fallen in love with you. I don't want to live without you. I want to have this baby with you and a few more, too. I want a houseful of kids. I don't ever want to go anyplace without you again. Not to Costa Rica or even to the corner drugstore. I want to marry you. Now."

She opened her mouth to speak, but he shook his head. "Don't say anything. You don't have to. I know what your answer is. You've made it clear to me. And I don't want you to say you love me, or marry me because you feel sorry for me." He took a deep breath. She was shocked. Too shocked to speak. "Now, what was it you had to tell me?"

She stared at him for a long moment before she answered. "It's about your car. It was totaled. That's the bad news. Your beautiful car."

He made a sound in his throat that was almost a laugh. "That's the good news," he said. "It wasn't my sports car. It was my new van."

"What? You bought a van?"

He nodded. "I traded the car in for a Eurovan. There's room for you, me and the baby and all the equipment. The stroller, the backpack, portable crib…"

"Joe…" Her eyes filled with tears. She bent over and kissed him lightly. "You traded in the car you loved for a van, a family van? You didn't need to do that."

"Yes, I did. I'm going to be a father. Of course it would be nice if I was a husband, too, if you'd marry me, but…"

"Oh, Joe." Claudia's eyes filled with tears. "Of course I'll marry you. I love you. I've always loved you. I don't know when it happened. If it was the night we worked all night getting out the annual report or the night of the Christmas party, but it feels like forever."

"It will be forever," he said.

Later, lying in his bed, looking out his window at the view of the bay, he was afraid it had all been a dream. She'd said yes. She'd told him she loved him. But had it really happened? When Claudia came into his room carrying a tray with his lunch and his medicine, dressed in jeans and a crisp white shirt knotted at the waist, he asked her.

"Did you really say you'd marry me?" he asked. "Or was that some drug-induced hallucination?"

She smiled and set the tray down on his dresser.

"I said it, and I meant it. So don't even think about blaming it on the medication. You're stuck with me," she said.

His whole body was flooded with relief. Claudia loved him. Claudia was going to marry him. He was going to be a father.

"As soon as I get well," he said. "We're getting married and we're going to make love. Not on a couch, not in a hurry, but here in this bed where we're going to stay until I've kissed every inch of your beautiful body and we've made love until you and I are both satiated, fulfilled and satisfied."

As it turned out, Joe Callaway kept his promise. The minute he was cleared by his doctor, they got married and made mad, passionate love in his bed. And he made his wife a very happy woman.

Epilogue

It was a beautiful day for a birthday party. The balloons at the end of the driveway signaled to the guests that this was the Callaway house. Even though Madison Callaway was only one year old, there were pony rides for the guests and a clown performing on the lawn. There was kid food, tiny finger sandwiches for the small guests and delicious small canapes for the grown-ups.

Claudia's friends Sharon and Al had brought their children, who made a beeline for the pizza cook in the white hat who was baking in the brick oven and handing out slices from a tray.

"I can't believe this," Sharon said, waving her hand around at the spacious lawn and patio, the swing set, the monkey bars and the playhouse that Madison was far too young yet to use. "It wasn't that long ago we first met Joe and you told me—correct me if I'm wrong, but didn't you tell me he was 'just a friend'?"

Claudia smiled guiltily. "I didn't mean to mislead you," she said. "I honestly thought that's all we were, just friends." Of course she'd known she hadn't wanted to be just a friend. She hadn't known she'd had a choice to be more.

"Of course, there's nothing wrong with marrying a friend," Sharon said.

"Not at all," Claudia said. "But I wanted more."

"Looks like you got it," Sharon said, beaming at Claudia's little girl. "And it looks like motherhood agrees with you."

"I confess I was worried," Claudia said. "That night at your house, it was Joe who bailed me out. It's Joe who's the natural father. He was great with your kids. I was the one who didn't know how to handle them."

"It's different when they're your own," Sharon said, watching Madison snuggle in the crook of her mother's neck.

"That's what Joe tried to tell me," she said. "It took some time for me to figure it out. And he's been great." She looked across the lawn to where

Joe was talking to his friends, looking as fit as ever in neatly pressed slacks and a navy polo shirt.

Just then their daughter spotted Joe, too.

"Da-da," Madison said, wriggling to get down. She ran on chubby, unsteady legs to her father who scooped her up in his arms and kissed her on the cheek.

Claudia's eyes filled with tears.

"I'm so lucky," she murmured. "I have Joe and the baby and…and…"

"And a never-ending supply of Callaway Coffee," Joe said, coming up behind her and kissing her on the nape of her neck. "What more could anyone want?"

*   *   *   *   *

From *USA TODAY* bestselling author

EMILIE RICHARDS

**comes the story of a woman who has played life
by the book, and now the rules have changed.**

Faith Bronson, daughter of a prominent Virginia senator and wife
of a charismatic lobbyist, finds her privileged life shattered when
her marriage ends abruptly. Only just beginning to face the lie
she has lived, she finds sanctuary with her two children in a
run-down row house in exclusive Georgetown. This historic
house harbors deep secrets of its own, secrets that force Faith
to confront the deceit that has long defined her.

PROSPECT STREET

"Richards adds to the territory
staked out by such authors as
Barbara Delinsky and Kristin Hannah....
Richards' writing is unpretentious and
effective and her characters burst with
vitality and authenticity."

—*Publishers Weekly*

*Available the first week of June 2003
wherever paperbacks are sold!*

MIRA®

eHARLEQUIN.com

Calling all aspiring writers!
Learn to craft the perfect romance novel
with our useful tips and tools:

- Take advantage of our **Romance Novel Critique Service** for detailed advice from romance professionals.

- Use our **message boards** to connect with writers, published authors and editors.

- Enter our **Writing Round Robin—** you could be published online!

- Learn many writing hints in our **Top 10 Writing lists!**

- **Guidelines** for Harlequin or Silhouette novels—what our editors *really* look for.

**Learn more about romance writing
from the experts—
visit www.eHarlequin.com today!**

If you enjoyed what you just read,
then we've got an offer you can't resist!

Take 2 bestselling
love stories FREE!
Plus get a FREE surprise gift!

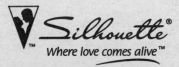

SILHOUETTE *Romance*®

COMING NEXT MONTH

#1672 COUNTERFEIT PRINCESS—Raye Morgan
Catching the Crown

When Crown Prince Marco Roseanova of Nabotavia discovered that Texas beauty Shannon Harper was masquerading as his runaway fiancée, he was furious—until he found himself falling for her. Still, regardless of his feelings, Marco had to marry royalty. But was Shannon really an impostor, or was there royal blood in her veins?

#1673 ONE BRIDE: BABY INCLUDED—Doreen Roberts

Impulsive, high-spirited Amy Richards stepped into George Bentley's organized life like a whirlwind on a quiet morning—chaotic and uninvited. George didn't want romance in his orderly world, yet after a few of this mom-to-be's fiery kisses…order be damned!

#1674 TO CATCH A SHEIK—Teresa Southwick
Desert Brides

Practical-minded Penelope Doyle didn't believe in fairy tales, and her new boss, Sheik Rafiq Hassan, didn't believe in love. But their protests were no guard against the smoldering glances and heart-stopping kisses that tempted Penny to revise her thinking…and claim this prince as her own.

#1675 YOUR MARRYING *HER?*—Angie Ray

Stop the wedding! Brad Rivers had always been Samantha Gillespie's best friend, so she certainly wasn't going to let him marry a woman only interested in his money! But was she ready to acknowledge the desire she was feeling for her handsome "friend" and even—gulp!—propose he marry *her* instead?

#1676 THE RIGHT TWIN FOR HIM—Julianna Morris

Was Patrick O'Rourke crazy? Maddie Jackson had sworn off romance and marriage, so why, after one little kiss, did the confirmed bachelor think she wanted to marry him? Still, beneath his I'm-not-the-marrying-kind-of-guy attitude was a man who seemed perfect as a husband and daddy.…

#1677 PRACTICE MAKES MR. PERFECT—
Patricia Mae White

Police Detective Brett Callahan thought he needed love lessons to lure the woman of his dreams to the altar, so he convinced neighbor Josie Matthews to play teacher. But none of his teachers had been as sweet and seductive as Josie, and *none* of their lessons had evoked passion like this!

SRCNM0603